THE MAGIC BICYCLE

The Story of a Bicycle That Found a Boy

JOHN BIBEE

Illustrated by Paul Turnbaugh

INTERVARSITY PRESS
DOWNERS GROVE, ILLINOIS 60515

InterVarsity Press is the book-publishing division of InterVarsity Christian Fellowship, a student movement active on campus at hundreds of universities, colleges and schools of nursing. For information about local and regional activities, write Public Relations Dept., InterVarsity Christian Fellowship, 6400 Schroeder Rd., P.O. Box 7895, Madison, WI 53707-7895.

Distributed in Canada through InterVarsity Press, 860 Denison St., Unit 3, Markham, Ontario L3R 4H1, Canada.

Cover illustration: Paul Turnbaugh

ISBN 0-87784-348-1

Printed in the United States of America

Library of Congress Cataloging in Publication Data

Bibee, John.
    The magic bicycle.

    Summary: The Spirit Flyer, a rusty old bicycle found in the city dump, surprises its new owner, John Kramar, when it magically lives up to its name, introducing John to an unknown world and changing his life for good.

    [1. Bicycles and bicycling—Fiction.   2. Fantasy]
I. Title.
PZ7.B471464Mag   1983   [Fic]   83-240
ISBN 0-87784-348-1

17	16	15	14	13	12	11	10	9	8	7	6	5
99	98	97	96	95	94	93	92	91	90	89		

For my mother and my father

THE BICYCLE THAT FOUND A BOY

· · · · · · · ·

1

Once there was a magic bicycle that found a boy. Although the boy didn't know it was magic at first, little by little he discovered some of the bicycle's secrets.

John Kramar was an ordinary boy who lived in Centerville. Because John's parents had died when he was very young, he lived with his Uncle Bill and Aunt Betty and their three daughters, Susan, Lois and Katherine. John usually liked living with his aunt and uncle and cousins; after being with them so many years, he felt as if they were the only family he had ever had. After all, he could barely remember his real parents.

John was honest and worked hard at school and at home. Most people liked him. But like all children, he had his faults, especially one that is common to many children his age. He was careless at times. He did things without thinking.

One spring day he was careless, and it cost him the new ten-speed bicycle that he had received for Christmas. While riding his bike home from school that day, he saw a darkly dressed man putting a poster in the toy-store window.

$$$

BICYCLE RACE!!! BICYCLE SAFETY CONTEST!!!

BEST-LOOKING BICYCLE CONTEST!!!

$$$$$$$$$$$$$$$$$$$$ CASH PRIZES!!! $$$$$$$$$$$$$$$$$$$$

$100, $75, $50 in each contest!

BIG DAY: FRIDAY, JUNE 6TH,

first day after school is out!

PLACE: CENTERVILLE SCHOOL!

Sponsored by Goliath Toys—

Giants of Fun, Fun, Fun!!!

$$$

John was so excited that he raced over to tell Roger Darrow the news. But when he got to Roger's house, instead of parking his bike on the front lawn, he left it in the driveway behind the Darrows' car.

While he was inside telling Roger the news, Roger's older brother

Rick got in the car and started to leave. Rick backed the car down the driveway. The noise was terrible. When they finally got the bike loose from under the car, it looked like a large blue and black pretzel with three bites taken out of it. The poor ten-speed was beyond repair.

No one needed to tell John that he'd been careless. When he took the bike home, his Uncle Bill just looked at it and shook his head sadly. John felt awful.

"I hope you aren't considering asking for another bicycle," Uncle Bill warned. "Sometimes I think you don't have any sense at all."

John looked down at his smashed bike, feeling the angry glare of his uncle. Susan, Lois and Katherine stood in a little silent circle around the broken bicycle. They felt bad too.

"I guess I was just too excited about telling Roger the news of the bike contests," John said weakly.

"Being excited is no excuse. You should know better. You'll have to make money to buy your next bicycle."

John almost began to cry. He had already felt bad about the bicycle, but now he felt even worse. Uncle Bill was the sheriff for Centerville. He was friendly to everyone and well respected for being fair. But if you broke the law, he was a hard man. Sometimes John felt as if his uncle was too much like a sheriff at home.

Fortunately, like a true friend, Roger shared his bike with John when he could. He even agreed to let John use his bike for the Safety Contest. But since only one person could ride Roger's bike in the race, John figured he'd be left on the sidelines watching someone else speed across the finish line.

One Sunday afternoon after dinner, about a week after John's bicycle was smashed, he and Roger rode out to the Centerville dump. They liked to go to the dump once in a while to see if there was any interesting trash. Roger had found a whole electric train set at the dump once. The engine didn't work, but after he and John tinkered with it a week and read books on electricity, they fixed it.

The dump was two miles out of town on a dirt road full of bumps and ruts. Roger let John ride on the handlebars until they went into a really big hole because Roger couldn't see with John sitting in front of him. John fell and Roger couldn't brake in time, so he jumped off. The bike landed on top of John's legs. The pedal sprocket ripped John's pants and cut a nasty gash in his leg. John limped the rest of the way to the dump, worried about what his uncle would say about the ripped pants.

The dump smelled worse than usual. It had rained the night before, and all the garbage was wet and moldy. But there was an even worse smell than the rotten garbage.

"Smells like something's dead, doesn't it?" Roger said. "Like a dead dog or cat."

"Yeah," John agreed, smelling the deadness.

Roger parked his bike and the boys began to explore. Feeling the pain in his leg, John was determined not to be careless again. He was especially careful as he stepped among the broken bottles, sharp tin cans and boards with nails. He used an old table leg to poke through the trash, where rats, snakes and spiders might be hiding.

In fact, John was trying to turn over an old smelly mattress when a large rat jumped out, ran between his feet and disappeared under a smashed cardboard box. John yelled out in surprise more than fear. Roger ran over.

"Just a rat," John said. He felt silly that his heart was beating so hard. Roger nodded, then pointed down at something. John saw it too.

Inside a hole in the mattress was a nest full of baby rats. The boys bent down for a better look. The baby rats, only a few days old, looked like squirming pieces of pink bubblegum covered with white fuzz.

"You must have scared the mother," Roger said.

"She sort of scared me too. I'm glad she wasn't hungry."

"She might come back. Think we should kill 'em?" He pointed at the nest of babies.

"Naw," John said. "Rats belong in a dump. They don't really hurt anything here. Besides, they're so little and . . . hey, look!"

Through another hole in the mattress John saw what looked like the spokes of a bicycle wheel. He pulled up a corner of the mattress slowly, not wanting to disturb the baby rats. Roger pulled off an old refrigerator door. It was a bicycle! Deep inside, John knew someone had answered his most secret wish. After pulling off an old chair and a busted crate of rotten lettuce, Roger grabbed the wheel and dragged the bicycle from the pile of trash. Suddenly he screamed.

John whirled around and saw his friend stumble backward, pointing at the bicycle. A large black snake was curled around the seat and stretched all the way to the handlebars. A horrible dead smell filled the air. John picked up the table leg and stepped toward the snake while Roger scrambled to his feet.

"Careful," Roger whispered. John didn't need to be reminded. The head of the snake, which had been resting on the handlebars, suddenly rose into the air, almost like a cobra. John stepped back.

"I've never seen a snake like that before," John said. On the snake's throat was a strange marking: a white X inside a white circle. John stared at the mysterious mark. A fear began to grow in him that he hadn't ever felt before. The dead smell seemed suffocating.

"I've never seen one like it either," Roger said. "I wonder if it's making that horrible smell? It's almost like it wants us to leave the bicycle alone."

"No," John said. "I want the bike. Maybe I can fix it up."

"But how are you going to . . ."

The snake hissed and flicked a blood-red tongue at John. Roger stepped back another step, but John stood still, staring into the angry red eyes. The snake seemed to be daring him to step closer. John raised his arm and with all his strength threw the table leg at the head of the snake. In a hiss of black lightning, the snake slithered off the bicycle, disappearing into the trash.

Both boys looked silently at the bike, amazed at how fast the snake had escaped. John suddenly felt himself breathe.

"Let's get away from the trash," John said, grabbing the handlebars. "He might still be close."

Roger helped John pull the bike about thirty feet away to a flat, clear place.

"At least we can see him if he comes back," Roger said, looking back at the junk pile. The snake with its circled X had scared him in an unusual way too. John looked back at the trash. He could still hear the strange way the snake hissed. The dead smell, which had been strong, lingered only faintly in the air.

"Well, let's see what we have," John said finally, turning to the rescued bicycle.

It seemed huge because it was an old, balloon-tire bicycle. Compared to Roger's thin, lightweight ten-speed, the old red bike seemed like a clumsy and rather ugly antique.

"What a mess," Roger said. "And it weighs a ton."

"It's not so bad," John said, hoping right away he could fix it up in time for the race and Safety Contest. With all the fixing in the world, John knew the bike would never win the Best-Looking Contest.

"But look at it," Roger said.

The old red bicycle did seem in sad shape. The big balloon tires looked as if they had been flat for years; the rubber was cracked and full of holes. Several of the spokes dangled. The thick frame, though basically straight, was full of dents and rusted spots. The handlebars were bent. The chain was rusted solid. A broken headlight stared off crookedly. An old rubber horn was rusted to the handlebars. When John squeezed the bulb, the air hissed weakly through two small holes in the rubber. Next to the right handgrip was a small gear-changing lever, connected to a cable which ran halfway down the frame, then ended, going nowhere. Near the other handgrip, an old rearview mirror hung upside down by one rusty bolt; all the glass was gone, except one small sliver stuck to the edge. On the rear wheel frame, an ancient light generator looked like a rusted metal bottle. The seat looked as if it had been chewed by two dozen rats; the springs beneath the seat were brittle from rust. The old fenders were mangled so badly they seemed beyond repair. But on the faded red middle bar of the frame, in curving white letters surrounded by a white border, the name remained—*Spirit Flyer*.

"What a mess," Roger repeated. "It looks like it's been through a war."

"Nothing's perfect," John said. "Besides, I need a bike."

"You don't mean you're going to try to fix that old thing?"

"I need a bike," John said again. "At least until I win the race and Safety Contest. Then I'll have enough money to buy a new bike."

"You're really dreaming," Roger said as John picked up the bike. The kickstand was rusted in the up position, so John held it steady, already figuring how he could make it rideable.

"It's not that heavy," John said, as he began pushing it. "It's *sturdy*, that's all." He grunted and pushed harder. The back flat tire skidded across the dirt.

"It won't even roll," Roger said. "I told you it was impossible."

"It's just the chain," John replied. "It's too stiff from rust. The back wheel can't turn."

John laid the bike down and walked back to the junk pile. A few moments later he returned with the broken handle of the refrigerator door. He carefully pushed the handle between the chain and the front sprocket. After five minutes of prying and tapping, he worked the chain off the front sprocket, then the rear sprocket, so the wheel was free to roll.

Even with the wheels rolling, the two-mile push back into town made John wonder if he should have left the old bike with the rest of the junk. His arms ached and he was covered with sweat by the time they reached his street.

"Oh, no," John groaned. Roger didn't have to ask why. Pedaling down the street toward them was Barry Smedlowe on his sleek new ten-speed, a smirk already spreading across his face. Barry rode by, staring at the old red bike, then circled around for another look.

"Where did you dig up that heap of junk? The dump's in the other direction," he whined, then began laughing. John and Roger almost covered their ears because Barry Smedlowe had a peculiar, high-pitched laugh that sounded like a sick donkey with hiccups. People avoided telling him jokes because of it. But that never stopped Barry. He liked to laugh, especially at things that weren't funny. He had tripped Roger when they were in fourth grade and went into hysterics even though Roger fell and sprained his arm. Since Roger couldn't prove that Barry had tripped him, Barry never got into trouble. Barry did things like that all the time, pulling chairs out from under people, yanking hair. And one of his favorite tricks was pulling out whatever he had in his nose and wiping it on other students' homework. But somehow he always avoided getting into trouble. He was just sneaky enough not to get caught. And if a teacher questioned him, he could lie for hours, looking as innocent as a kitten. Since Barry's father was the school principal, the teachers didn't want problems. Barry was always declared innocent.

"We just came from the dump," Roger said. "Why would we want to go back?"

"Ssshhhh," John whispered to Roger, but it was too late.

"I knew it!" Barry screeched. "A dump bike for the dummy. Hey, dumpy boy. Dumper! Ha, haaaaaaaaaagh!"

John just kept pushing the old bike, a bit upset at Roger for telling Barry it came from the dump. Even though Roger was his best friend, he thought Roger talked too much at times. He also felt embarrassed because the bike *did* look old and ugly next to Barry and Roger's bikes.

"It sort of looks like a fat old cow with arthritis, Dumper," Barry yelled. "Is that a new form of exercise, bike pushing? You're sweating like a pig. Probably smell as bad as that garbage bike you got there."

John stopped. When John stopped, Barry stopped pedaling, afraid to get any closer. Even though Barry was older and bigger, he didn't like to fight unless he had his gang, the Cobra Club, with him. Right after Christmas, Barry had started the Cobra Club. Barry was the president, vice president and treasurer. Each member had to pay dues every month to Barry. Besides that, they had to paint their bicycles black and put a special decal of a cobra's head on the front, right below the handlebars. On special occasions, the Club members wore black pants and black jackets with an emblem of a cobra's head with its mouth open, the fangs oozing a drop of poison.

John had been the first person Barry had asked to join his club, but John refused. He didn't want to be in a club with Barry as the dictator, telling everyone what to do. Six boys did join. One of the advantages was that Club members could swim in the Smedlowes' swimming pool. And Mrs. Smedlowe always had cookies, potato chips, ice cream and sodas for the Club meetings. John thought Barry was just buying friends because he couldn't make any by himself. And one time he told the whole Cobra Club that he thought the black pants and jackets made them look like undertakers. All the other kids laughed and began calling them the Dead Men's Club. Ever since then Barry had held a grudge against John and his friends, trying to think of ways to get even.

But John knew he wouldn't try anything without his gang. After John stopped pushing the old bike, he turned and stared calmly at Barry. Barry looked nervous, then brayed out a laugh, stopping short when he saw the serious expression on John's face.

"By the way, I heard your poor little bike got run over," Barry said, mimicking a baby's voice.

"I thought of calling your undertaker club to help me bury it," John said, then smiled sweetly at the bigger boy. Roger laughed and so did John as a dark frown spread across Barry's face. He raised his hand and shook his finger at John.

"You watch out who you're calling names," Barry said through clenched teeth, "or you won't even have that junk heap of a bike to ride. We have ways of dealing with a smart mouth like you."

John laughed at the bigger boy's threat, then began pushing the old red bike again. Suddenly a rock thudded into John's back. John turned and charged, but Barry was already pedaling away. John saw that it was useless, especially since his leg still hurt from the cut. Roger jumped on his bike and pedaled after the fleeing loudmouth. Barry rounded the corner with Roger gaining on him. Then the bikes disappeared behind a house. John picked up the Spirit Flyer and pushed it the rest of the way home.

FIXING
THE SPIRIT
FLYER
· · · · · · · ·

2

The first thing John did once he got the bicycle home was close the garage door so no one could see him working. He could still hear Barry's biting words about having an old ugly bike. The bike was a mess, John had to admit, but he also pictured how nice the bike would look once he fixed it up. At least he hoped it would look ok.

Using pliers, a big screwdriver and a lot of rust-dissolving oil, John loosened the kickstand so it would come down. Now the bike stood on its own so John could use both hands to work on the other problems.

He took off the old broken headlight, the horn, the gear-changing lever, the mirror and the generator. Although John couldn't have known it then, this was a mistake. The light, horn, mirror, gear-changing lever and generator were not ordinary bicycle instruments, but magic ones. John almost threw them into the trash can, but he suddenly got a feeling that he should keep them. He dropped them into an old cardboard box, put them on a shelf in the garage and forgot about them until much later.

While John was working on the rusty chain, he heard a knock on the garage door. He peeked out the window and saw Roger. Opening the door just a crack, he let Roger in.

"He got away," Roger said. "I just about had him when he got to his house. I thought he was going to knock down the front door trying to get in before I grabbed him. Then he made faces out the window. He's real brave when his mother's standing behind him."

John nodded. Barry Smedlowe always went crying to his parents whenever he was in trouble. They never seemed to realize their good boy could do anything wrong.

Roger helped John make the rusty chain flexible again. For an hour they tugged and tapped, using lots of rust-dissolving oil. John cut his hand on a sharp edge and the oil burned in the wound, but he kept working anyway. After the chain was ready, they put it back on the sprockets. John turned the bicycle upside-down and pushed the pedals. The back wheel turned now. It was a little wobbly, but ok. John spun the front wheel with his hand. Although it squeaked and a few of the loose spokes clicked against the frame, the wheel was in good shape.

While Roger removed the fenders and wheels to work on the loose spokes and flat tires, John got a piece of sandpaper from the workbench to work on the rust. Wherever there was a dent, there was rust. He knew that he had to fight the rust, that the metal had to be clean and spotless, or else it would rust again.

John worked the rest of the afternoon sanding and sanding some more. Roger had to go home for supper before John was finished, so John worked alone, turning on the light when it got dark. He was working so hard that he didn't even hear his three cousins come into the garage to watch him. The girls, who were really like sisters to him, watched quietly. Katherine, who was only five, was the first to speak.

"What is it?" she asked in her little squeaky voice.

"A *bi*cycle, of course," said Lois. She was seven and thought she was much wiser than Katherine. "I *think* it's a bicycle."

"Sure it's a bicycle," said Susan, who was twelve, a year older than John. "See, the wheels are leaning against the wall."

"Oh, yes," said Katherine. "I guess it is a bicycle. Look at John. He looks like Mr. Fenly."

John stopped working, standing up to stretch. Mr. Fenly owned a garage and was always greasy from working underneath cars all day.

"He's worse than Mr. Fenly," Lois said. "I hope you aren't wearing your good clothes, or you know what Mom and Dad will say."

"What will Mom say?" asked John's aunt as she stepped through the door followed by Uncle Bill. She stared at John. "Oh, John! Look at you!"

John looked down at himself. His jeans, which had been blue earlier, were splotched with grease and oil. His shirt and face were equally dirty.

"These are old clothes," John said weakly, realizing he should have been more careful.

"They can be classified as *very* old clothes now," Uncle Bill said, frowning and shaking his head. "Sometimes I think you don't have a brain, John. You know the rules about working in old clothes. Why can't you be more careful?"

John looked down at the floor. Rules, rules, rules, he thought, but he didn't say anything. He knew his clothes were ruined; the grease and oil stains would never wash out.

"Where did you find the bike?" his uncle asked. "Looks like you're doing a good repair job."

John looked up. Uncle Bill was trying to be nice. He was angry about John's clothes, but he wouldn't stay angry.

"I found it at the dump," John said.

"The dump?" Lois asked. "Don't you throw things away at the dump?"

"It's a really nice old bike," John said quickly. "Right now it doesn't look so great, but just wait till I'm through. It'll work. You'll see."

"Well, it's time for supper," Aunt Betty said, stlll frowning at John's clothes.

"Can't I eat later?" John asked. "Please? I don't have much more to do, and I'll have to get cleaned up, then dirty again. Please?"

Mrs. Kramar looked at her husband. He sighed. Uncle Bill had a strict rule about the family eating together, especially supper. That was the time each person shared what had happened that day.

"I guess we can make an exception in this case," Uncle Bill said. "But it's an exception. What kind of bike is it, anyway?" He turned his head sideways, trying to read the writing upside-down.

"It's a Spirit Flyer," John said.

Uncle Bill stiffened. A disturbed expression appeared on his face. He stared at the words, painted on the bike's framc, then looked at his wife. She put her hand over her mouth as if she were afraid. She stared back at her husband.

"Is anything wrong?" John asked, seeing the sudden change that had come over his aunt and uncle.

Neither said a word for a moment. They stared at the old bicycle, then back at each other.

"Nothing's wrong," Aunt Betty said finally. "But don't even come into the house with your clothes like that. You say you found that bike at the dump?"

"Yes," John said. Another worried look passed between his aunt and uncle, but they said nothing. Uncle Bill shrugged, then went inside the house. Aunt Betty followed.

John grabbed the sandpaper and returned to the rust spots. He was so busy, he didn't notice his cousins leave.

He was almost through with the last of the sanding when Susan came into the garage with a hamburger, a pile of potato chips and a glass of milk.

"Dad grilled hamburgers," she said. "I made yours with pickles and mustard, the way you like 'em."

"Thanks," John replied. He wiped his dirty hands on his even dirtier pants and began eating the food. Susan, who had changed into her old work clothes, picked up a piece of sandpaper and finished sanding where John had stopped. John drained the glass of milk, then looked for some red paint.

Susan helped John mix two kinds of red paint to match the red color of the bicycle. With two small brushes they worked together, painting over all the sanded spots.

"Maybe we should just paint the whole thing," John said, though he dreaded the idea of sanding another inch.

"No, it looks fine," Susan said. "Besides, you wouldn't want to paint over its name. I like the name Spirit Flyer. It sounds majestic."

John nodded, more because he was tired and didn't want to work anymore that night. Majestic or not, the Spirit Flyer looked better than it had when he brought it home.

"Did you notice the way Mom and Dad acted when they saw the name?" Susan asked.

"Yeah," John said, remembering the odd way his uncle looked at Aunt Betty.

"Well, they acted kind of funny during supper too."

"What did they say?"

"It wasn't what they said, but just how they acted, sort of," she said slowly, trying to find the right words. "Dad seemed upset during supper. And later, when they were in the kitchen, I heard Mom say something, but I couldn't hear what it was exactly. The tone of her voice was strange. Then Dad said, 'It's not possible. It's probably a coincidence.' I went into the kitchen then, and they stopped talking and looked at me sort of funny. I got the idea that whatever they were talking about was a secret, like hiding Christmas toys or surprise parties, only this wasn't fun stuff."

"Who knows?" John said. "But it must not be anything bad about the bike or they wouldn't let me keep it. They must have been thinking of something else."

"Probably," Susan said, staring at the old bicycle, still glistening in the fresh paint. "What about tires?"

"I'll have to buy new tires and inner tubes," John said. "I hope they don't cost too much."

"I think it will be a nice bike," Susan said. "Even if it is a little old."

John cleaned the paintbrushes and tools while Susan got him clothes he could wear into the house. Just before turning off the light, he stared at the old red bike sitting upside-down, the flat tires leaning against the wall. He wondered if he could win the race on a bike so heavy and old.

"I can only try," he said to himself, then turned out the light.

Right after school on Monday, John and Roger ran to the hardware store to buy new tires and inner tubes. John barely had enough money to buy the twenty-six-inch tires and tubes.

"Don't sell many of this type anymore," Mr. Crenshaw said. He owned the hardware store.

John and Roger ran all the way to John's house. With the garage door closed, John slipped the inner tubes over the rims of the wheels. He was extra careful not to hurt the valve stems as he pushed them through their holes in the wheels. He had ruined an inner tube once by poking a hole in the valve stem; it had been impossible to patch.

"What about these?" Roger asked, holding up the old inner tubes. John took them and pulled them. The rubber was still stretchy. He dropped them into the box that held the old broken light and other gadgets he had taken off the bicycle.

"Maybe I can use the inner tubes for patches," John said. Roger agreed.

Even though he was anxious to take the old red bike on a trial run, he slowly put on the tires, making sure the inner tube wasn't pinched on an edge. Roger had the air pump ready. John pumped up the back tire; Roger pumped up the front. Using his uncle's tire gauge, John tested the air pressure. He had to let a little air out of the back tire before it was ready.

John checked the nuts on the wheel to make sure they were tight. Then using his uncle's biggest wrench, they straightened the handlebars. John was in such a hurry by that time that he made one mistake. Though he had straightened the handlebars, he forgot to retighten the bolt that allowed the handlebars to move up and down.

John threw the wrench on the workbench, flung open the garage door and pushed the Spirit Flyer outside. As the bike coasted down the driveway, John jumped onto the seat and began to pedal.

"It works!" John yelled as he pedaled in a circle in the street. Roger hopped on his bike and sprinted down the street. Because the Spirit Flyer was a heavier bike, it was harder for John to work up speed. Roger used the lower gears on his light-weight ten-speed and shot out ahead. But John kept pedaling hard, and by the time he was at cruising speed, he caught up with Roger. The two boys breezed around the corner and headed for Crofts Road where they could ride without worrying about cars.

They hadn't gone two blocks before they saw Barry Smedlowe and his gang, the Cobra Club, pedaling toward them on their black bicycles. Barry was pedaling standing up. John and Roger realized at the same time that Barry didn't intend to move as he got closer. He was challenging them in a game called chicken. Two people would pedal straight at each other, and whoever moved at the last minute was the chicken. John,s aunt and uncle had forbidden him to play chicken, but it wasn't a game John liked anyway. He thought it was stupid and dangerous. But it was just the type of game Barry Smedlowe liked. Barry had a horrible grin on his face as he raced closer.

At the last instant, Roger and John swerved to the outside as Barry sped by between them screaming, "Chickeeeeeeeen!" The rest of the

Cobra Club hooted as they whizzed by, following Barry.

John and Roger tried to ignore Barry and his gang, but they were hard to ignore. They circled around, then sped up until they were just behind Roger and John.

"Afraid that old junk heap of a bike won't hold up in a little game of chicken?" Barry taunted, staying just far enough away to make a quick escape if needed. John and Roger looked straight ahead, ignoring the bigger boy's words.

"I'm surprised that dump heap even rolls, Dumper," Barry said, pedaling a little closer to John. The Cobra Club members laughed. "You aren't thinking of entering it in the race, are you?"

"Of course he's going to race it," Roger said. "We'll beat you."

"Oh, really," said Barry. "I'll race you chickens to Crofts Road right now. Ready, set, go!"

Barry stood up on his pedals and sprinted out ahead. Roger took off after him and was followed by the members of the Cobra Club. John was last. Barry had a long lead at first, but Roger was gaining on the bigger boy. John, on the heavier old red bike, was behind, trying with all his might to catch up. He was finally cruising fast, about twenty feet behind the other boys when he heard a clicking noise from the Spirit Flyer's rear wheel. John looked down while trying to keep up his speed. A spoke had come loose and was knocking against the frame each time the wheel turned around. Instead of stopping, which would have been the wise thing to do, John kept racing, looking back at the loose spoke, trying to think of a solution.

But you should never look backward very long while pedaling a bicycle. Without knowing it, John had swerved toward the side of the road and was heading straight toward a parked car. Fortunately he looked up in time to see the car, but unfortunately he was going too fast to stop. He jerked the old bike to the right, just missing the rear fender of the car. But because he was going so fast, the Spirit Flyer went into a skid, sliding across the loose gravel on the street. John stomped on the brake, but it was too late. He hit the ground and slid underneath the old red bike. A stab of pain shot through his hand and leg as the bike hit the street in a crunching clatter.

John was still sitting on the road, examining a cut in his leg and the burning scrape on his hand, when Roger rode up and stopped.

"You ok?" Roger asked.

"I think so," John replied, grunting as he tried to stand up. "I turned around when I heard you wreck," Roger said.

"So he won. And here they come to gloat."

They could hear Barry's braying laugh a block away. He coasted past slowly, laughing hysterically when he saw John's hand and leg were bleeding. His gang grinned like a group of monkeys.

"What's the matter?" Barry said in a baby voice. "Did the little boy fall off his tricycle?" He thought this was funny and began another roaring laugh. John bent down to tie his shoe.

"You better get training wheels for that garbage heap if you want to race," Barry said, then pedaled slowly away, his laughter stinging John's ears. John waited until the Cobra Club was out of sight before saying anything.

"I guess I better take this dump-heap bike home," John said bitterly. "What's the use?" He kicked the tire of the Spirit Flyer, then got on. Roger didn't say anything, but pedaled alongside his friend.

When they got to John's house, Roger asked if he wanted to fix the loose spoke. John said no. He shoved the bike against the garage wall and knocked down the kickstand. Knowing that John wanted to be alone, Roger rode home.

For a long time John just stared at the old red bike, hating its heaviness and ugliness. Even painted, it was still ugly and fat-looking compared to everyone else's bicycle. John slammed the garage door.

"I'll never ride you again," John said to the old red bike. "You're just a garbage-heap bike. I should have left you with the rest of the trash."

John slammed the door as he went into the house.

THE MAGIC
IN THE
BICYCLE
· · · · · · · · ·

3

John didn't ride the bike for two days. Even though it was his own fault that he'd been careless and hadn't watched where he was going, he blamed the wreck on the bike. Like many people, he was slow to admit that he'd made a mistake. Every time he felt the pain in his leg or saw the scab on his hand, he felt a little surge of anger toward the Spirit Flyer. He was sorry he had spent his money for the tires, money he could have saved to buy a good new bike.

On Thursday after school, Susan asked John if she could have the bike, since he wasn't riding it. John told her he might sell it since he had spent money for the tires. Susan asked how much money he wanted.

John was tempted to name a price. But the fact that Susan wanted the bike made him think again. He wasn't sure he really wanted to get rid of the Spirit Flyer. Even if he sold it, he wouldn't have enough money for a new bike, or even a good used one. He still wanted to enter the race and Safety Contest. By now John realized that it wasn't the bike's fault that he crashed but his own.

After Susan offered to buy the bike, John went into the garage for another look. The Spirit Flyer was still leaning against the wall where he'd left it, the loose spoke dangling from the back wheel. John stared at the bike for a long time, then quietly got a pair of pliers and began fixing the spoke. Without anyone to hear him, John spoke two words to the old bike. "I'm sorry," he said quietly.

John put the pliers away, then hopped on the bike. He pedaled down the alleys and back streets, trying to avoid his friends. He pedaled out to Crofts Road, then began going faster. He worked up to cruising speed slowly because both his legs still hurt from his accidents. But once he really got going, the bike whizzed down the road at tremendous speed. John realized he might still have a chance for the race if he practiced enough. The ten-speed bicycles had a big advantage in getting off to quicker starts than the old single-speed Spirit Flyer. He knew he would have to make up for this handicap somehow if he was going to win the race.

John pedaled down Crofts Road until he came to the dump road. Since there were still two hours until supper, he decided to ride out toward the dump. That way he could practice in total privacy.

He pedaled across the ancient wooden bridge over the Sleepy Eye River. After the bridge, the dirt road to the dump began. John rode on the edge of the road to avoid the long ruts and the large holes. He didn't want another accident. He was already worried that his legs might still be sore by the time of the bike race, three weeks away.

Even though John was determined to be careful and avoid all the bumps, he couldn't help but look when off to his right he saw what looked like a deer. Instead of stopping the bike, he only slowed down while he searched for the animal. Just when he saw the beautiful doe and fawn, it happened.

The bike had slowly swerved toward the center of the road, straight into a deep rut. When John felt the tire going down, he jerked the handlebars, trying to avoid falling into the rut. But he was too late. The tire hit the bottom hard, so hard it jarred his teeth.

But a strange thing happened at that moment. When the bike started down into the hole, it threw John forward over the front of the handlebars. John held on as hard as he could, which saved him from another bad accident. But because he had forgotten to tighten the handlebars the day he fixed the bike, they bent down under his weight. In fact, the handlebars bent down so far that John almost bumped his chin when he lost his balance. At the same time the bike hit the end of the rut, the front tire jumped into the air as if the bike were being shot off a small ramp.

John knew he was bound to crash when the bike came back down because he was already hanging over the handlebars. But the front tire didn't come back down. It kept going up into the air, one foot, two feet, then three feet off the ground. And not only that, the back tire came out of the rut and left the ground also. The old red bike seemed to be shooting right up into the sky!

John jerked back in fear, screaming and pulling on the handlebars, trying to stop. He pulled so hard that the loose handlebars came back up, this time too high. At that instant, the bike dipped back toward the ground. The front tire gently landed on the old dirt road, followed by the rear tire. John pushed the handlebars back down so they were level and pushed down hard on the brake. The bike stopped. He hopped off and put the kickstand down. As he stood there trying to catch his breath, he stared at the old red bicycle, wondering what happened.

He wasn't surprised that the wheel had left the ground when it hit the end of the rut. That was normal. He and Roger had jumped their bikes off ramps in the past a lot of times. But this had been different.

The front tire had been three or more feet off the ground and showed no signs of coming down when he jerked the handlebars up. And the back tire had been almost as far off the ground. Even at his fastest speed, his old bicycle had never gone anywhere near that high off the ground . . . or for such a long distance.

John ran back to the rut. He could see his tire tracks swerve into the rut, and his wobbly tracks inside the rut. But then the tracks ended and didn't start again for twenty feet. John whistled. Even at his fastest he'd never traveled farther than five or six feet. But he hadn't even been going fast when he came out of the rut. John looked at the old red bicycle leaning on its kickstand. He tried to remember exactly what happened.

After thinking things over for several minutes, he knocked the kickstand up and got back on the curious old bicycle. He pedaled past a series of bumps in the road looking for a smooth stretch. Finally he came to a place free of holes and ruts. John slowed down, gulped, then carefully pushed down on the handlebars. They didn't move. He pushed harder until the handlebars began to bend. At the moment they started to bend, the front wheel lifted off the ground. John watched the wheel rise higher and higher, one foot, then two feet off the ground. John was afraid to look back at the rear tire, but he felt it leave the road too.

When the Spirit Flyer's front tire was about waist high off the ground, John became scared that he would fall off the old red bike. But he didn't panic. Instead, he pulled the handlebars up until they pointed down. The moment they pointed down, the bicycle began going down. The front tire touched the ground softly, followed by the rear tire. John leveled the handlebars and stopped.

He was breathing hard with excitement, but he told himself not to be careless. He began pedaling the old red bicycle again. He immediately pushed the loose handlebars down. The front tire went up into the air just as before. John glanced back just in time to see the rear wheel leave the ground too. This time he waited until the bike was head high off the ground before pulling up on the handlebars. But instead of pulling the handlebars all the way up, he only pulled them up until they were level, as they should be normally. The front tire stopped rising the instant John pulled the handlebars level. But this time the Spirit Flyer didn't dip back to the ground. Instead, it flew through the air level with the road about five feet off the ground. He pedaled slowly, waiting to see if the bike would drop. As long as the handlebars were straight, the old red bike traveled through the air at the same height.

John flew above the old dump road for almost a hundred yards, then pulled the handlebars up. Instantly the Spirit Flyer began to descend. The bike landed and John braked to a stop.

John stared far down the road to make sure there were no low-hanging tree limbs, then started pedaling. He pushed down on the handlebars, and the bike took off into the air. But this time John let the Spirit Flyer climb until it was as high as the roof of his house before pulling the handlebars level. The old red bike traveled along high off the ground. John began to pedal faster and the Spirit Flyer jumped forward.

When he saw the low-hanging tree limbs, he pulled the handlebars up. As he expected, the bike went down, down, down and landed on the dirt road. John didn't stop this time but kept pedaling until he passed the trees. When his path was clear, he pointed the handlebars up and the old red bike took off. If he hadn't been so excited, he would have seen a long black snake lying in the road just where the wheels of the old red bicycle left the ground. John smelled a terrible odor of something dead, but he didn't think about it. The black snake rose up into the air, its red eyes staring at the flying bicycle and boy. The white circled X on the snake's throat spread out as the snake hissed, its red tongue flicking into the air.

John let the Spirit Flyer rise until it was above the trees before leveling off. Once he could look down on the top of the tallest tree, the boy began to pedal faster. The speed of the old red bike increased more than

he expected. The bike whizzed through the air, slightly humming as the wind sped by.

Seeing a flat cow pasture off to his left, John decided to try another experiment. He turned the bike to his left and the bike flew out over the pasture. John turned to the right, and the bike flew to the right. High in the sky above the pasture, John traveled in a large circle. Riding the Spirit Flyer seemed to be the same as riding a regular bicycle, only it was much smoother as it glided through the air. But not only could it fly, it took less effort to go fast. John didn't have to pedal hard to reach the fastest speed he could go on the ground. And when he pedaled even faster, because it was so easy to pedal in the air, the bike went as fast as a motorcycle or car. John hadn't even begun to go as fast as he could pedal before he became scared and decided to slow down. He stepped back on the brake, and the bike slowed to a normal bicycle speed.

Using the brake made John wonder if he would fall out of the sky if he completely stopped the bike. He knew that on the ground it was almost impossible to keep a bike balanced if it wasn't moving. To test it out, John flew back until he saw a flat place in the cow pasture. He pointed the Spirit Flyer down and slowly approached the ground. When he was only about one foot above the grassy pasture, he leveled off and stepped on the brake until the bike slowed to an absolute stop and then lowered slowly to the ground. John noticed he didn't have any trouble keeping his balance as the bike descended.

Once he landed, he began pedaling and pointed the bike up. As before, he leveled the bike off at a foot above the pasture. When he braked, the bike slowed to a stop, then began dropping. But this time John took his foot off the brake. The bike stopped moving and stood in the air, perfectly still, six inches above the ground. The most amazing thing to John was that he had no trouble keeping his balance; it was the same as sitting in a chair. He sat for a minute, hanging above the ground, then pressed on the brake. The bicycle dropped until it softly landed.

John took the bicycle up again, leveling off at about tree height. He hit the brake and the bicycle stopped as before, then slowly started dropping toward the ground. John took his foot off the brake, and as before, the bike hung motionless in the air, twenty feet above the cow pasture. The boy sat high in the sky, feeling like a king with the world beneath him.

John whooped with joy and began pedaling, guiding the Spirit Flyer up above the trees. He went so high that even the trees seemed tiny below him. The old dump road looked like a tiny brown ribbon until it reached the tiny bridge. Beyond the bridge, John could see Crofts Road running into Centerville. The town looked like the tiny toy town that surrounded the electric train set that Roger kept in his basement. John could see cars moving in the streets. He could even pick out the roof of his house as he pedaled closer.

But John didn't pedal too close to the town. At first he wanted to fly straight to his house, circle above the roof, and yell until his aunt and uncle came outside and saw him. Then he would land magnificently in the back yard. But as he pedaled closer to the town, he got a strong feeling that he should wait, that it might not be a good idea to go flying over Centerville like a boy on a rocket. John circled back toward the dump, deciding to keep the magic of the Spirit Flyer a secret, at least for a while.

John practiced flying, losing all track of time. Suddenly he noticed it was darker; the sun had dipped below the horizon. And far off, approaching the town, he saw a mass of angry dark clouds. Rain clouds. John sped through the air, dropping lower and lower, until he was only three feet off the ground by the time he reached the bridge over the Sleepy Eye River. He landed on the bridge, then rode the Spirit Flyer like a regular bicycle down Crofts Road. He could barely keep himself from taking the old red bike up into the air again. But something told him not to fly. He pedaled at his top ground speed all the way into town.

The sky was black with clouds by the time he reached his house. He parked the Spirit Flyer in the garage, making sure it was out of the way. Then he went inside.

As soon as he opened the door he smelled supper. For a moment he hoped he wasn't too late. But his hopes faded as he walked into the living room and saw Susan clearing away the dishes. Uncle Bill looked at him sternly.

"You're an hour late, John," he said. "Where have you been?"

"Riding the Spirit Flyer," John said. "I'm sorry I'm late."

"Sorry's not enough," his uncle said. "You know the rules. What's the rule for a late supper?"

"Stay in the yard for a week," John said. "But can't we make an exception? I mean, I didn't mean to be late. I just was . . ."

"Rules are rules," Uncle Bill said. "If you start breaking all the house rules, wanting exceptions, what do I say to the girls? Is it fair for you to break the rules and not them?"

"No, sir," John said.

"If you start breaking all the rules, your life will be one big shambles. You will never accomplish anything."

"Yes, sir," John said. He knew there was no use in arguing. But knowing he would have to stay in the yard all week, right after discovering the Spirit Flyer's secret, was almost more than he could bear.

"How does that old bike work?" Uncle Bill asked.

"Ok," John said without enthusiasm. "It really flies."

If he had looked up, John would have seen the nervous glance that passed between his aunt and uncle. But John could only think how much of a prison the house would be for a whole week. He looked down at his clean plate on the table. Rules, rules, rules, he thought. Rules for supper, rules for keeping his bedroom clean, rules for work, rules for play. Why does my uncle have so many rules, rules, rules?

Outside the sky was dark. Suddenly, lightning split the sky in an angry flash. A low rumble of thunder followed. Rain began hitting the roof.

THE
RAIN AND
MR. GRINSBY

4

The house wasn't so bad a prison as John expected because of the rain. It started that night, right after supper, a slow but steady rain. And it didn't stop. For nine days it rained on Centerville. Though there had been harder rains, no one around town could ever remember its lasting so long. But the strangest thing was that it rained only on Centerville and the surrounding area. Towns twenty miles away didn't receive a drop. The Sleepy Eye River flooded, which it hadn't done for seven years, and washed away three bridges around the town, including the old dump road bridge. The people on the other side of the river, mostly farmers, had to travel twenty miles south to cross the river if they wanted to go to Centerville.

The rain made Uncle Bill uneasy. As sheriff he had a lot more work and problems because of the rain and floods. People called into the office every hour complaining about leaking roofs or overflowing sewer pipes or wrecked bridges, as if he could fix everything by himself in five minutes. But the calls that bothered him the most were the reports of funnel clouds, tornado clouds. Centerville was not in an area which normally had tornadoes. Yet every day during the rain people would call in, saying they had spotted a big black funnel cloud east of town, or west or north, or moving closer to town. But Sheriff Kramar never saw one.

The constant reports worried him. During the long rain of seven years ago, the last time the Sleepy Eye had flooded, there were also reports of tornado clouds. But the tornadoes, if they really were tornadoes, never destroyed anything, except possibly one car which had been found twisted and mangled. That car had belonged to John's parents.

Sheriff Kramar was still haunted by that long rain. John's father had reported seeing tornado clouds, but he said they weren't really tornadoes, but something else. Sheriff Kramar found his brother's wrecked car, but John's parents weren't in it. The whole town searched the area, but never found a clue. Sheriff Kramar assumed they were dead. He told John his parents had died in a car accident. John was only four years old when he moved in with his uncle's family. He was too young to remember much about the long rain or the stories about tornadoes. All he knew was that his parents were gone.

Sheriff Kramar was in his office talking on the phone about a broken sewer pipe when he saw a black-suited man coming up the steps through the rain. When he came into the office, he snapped down his umbrella, shaking water all over the floor. George, Uncle Bill's deputy and radio dispatcher, groaned when he saw the water. He had just mopped. He turned his wheelchair around and rolled over to the closet to get the mop again. The man paid no attention to him.

"Sheriff," the man said, tipping his derby, showing his orange-red hair. He acted as if he had known Sheriff Kramar for twenty years. "Horace Grinsby of Goliath Toys. Remember? The bicycle race, Safety Contest and Best-Looking Bike Contest which will grace your fair town the day after the delightful children leave school for the summer?"

"Yes, of course," Uncle Bill said, shaking Grinsby's hand. What a limp handshake, the sheriff thought to himself. Like shaking hands with a corpse. Grinsby kept grinning, but his smile seemed painted on, like one on a puppet. When most people smile they have happy eyes. But Grinsby's pale, reddened eyes were eyes that only watched.

"The reason for my visit is that I need some more posters approved announcing the contests," Grinsby said. He produced a long cardboard tube from beneath his black suit coat. It contained the same kind of posters that John had seen in the toy-store window.

"No problem," Sheriff Kramar said. "Will you stamp these, George?" The young deputy wheeled over and took the posters.

"I have one other small request, Sheriff," Grinsby said, grinning even more broadly. "Will you be so kind as to judge the Safety Contest? As the man of authority in this town, you know the rules of bicycle safety better than anyone, I dare say. Would you do me that favor?"

"Yes, of course," Sheriff Kramar said. "Unless I get called away that morning by an emergency. You'll need to get a back-up judge."

"Certainly, certainly," Grinsby nodded rapidly. "I thought of approaching the school principal, a Mr. Smedlowe. After all, the contests and race will take place on school property. And a grand day it will be. A grand day! Yessir. Goliath Toys, Giants of Fun, Fun, Fun, our motto, will be honored to hold these contests in the fair burg of Centertown."

"Centerville," Sheriff Kramar corrected.

"Yes, of course, Centerville," Grinsby said, his smile stretching to his ears. "How utterly silly of me. Well, it's been a long day. And such nasty weather. I could have sworn I saw a tornado cloud this morning. Gave me quite a fright."

"Yes, well, I need to be checking on some bridge repairs, if you'll excuse me, Mr. Grinsby." Sheriff Kramar put on his raincoat and hat and went outside. Grinsby tipped his derby, opened his umbrella and followed the sheriff out the door.

After distributing his posters all over town, Grinsby went to a small black truck with "Goliath Toys, Giants of Fun! Fun! Fun!" painted on the steep sides of the back. Grinsby slammed the door and, making sure no one was watching, pulled aside the black curtain that separated the cab from the rest of the truck. He picked up a red telephone, dialed three numbers, then began to talk in a whisper.

"I haven't located it yet," he said. For once he wasn't grinning. "This contest thing should bring it out. The rain is perfectly miserable."

Grinsby laughed, as if he somehow enjoyed a rainstorm that made the residents of Centerville suffer. He listened for a moment, then smiled, laughing at what he heard.

"Why not?" he said. "A little fire always makes things more interesting. Besides, it might work. We could speed the plan up."

Grinsby listened some more, then put the telephone away. He stared out into the falling rain. Suddenly, far away, a long flash of lightning split the sky, followed by a loud clap of thunder.

Grinsby began to laugh again.

FIRE
AT THE
McCRADLES'

5

John stared out at the drizzling rain. His punishment had ended on Thursday and he was anxious to ride the Spirit Flyer, but the rain continued, with the lightning storms. There had already been one fire in town; a telephone pole had been struck by lightning and burst into flames. All the telephones in two blocks were out for a whole night.

The boy saw that the rain made his uncle nervous, but he didn't understand exactly why. Aunt Betty had told John and his cousins that Uncle Bill just had more problems when it rained, and that was why he acted so worried. On Friday night after supper, John and his cousins put on a small play for Uncle Bill. Aunt Betty made popcorn balls and hot chocolate. Everyone was having a good time until Uncle Bill had to leave on an emergency call south of town.

The rain continued slow and steady on Saturday morning. John was tired of staying in the house, so he went down to the sheriff's office with his uncle.

John liked the station and everyone there liked him. He especially liked to play chess or checkers with George. John felt sorry for him because he was confined to a wheelchair. But George never complained; he and John were good friends.

John and George were deep into a chess game when the phone rang. George answered.

"What?" George asked. "What? I can't hear you. Slow down . . . What? . . . But hold on—"

Looking puzzled, George hung up the phone.

"I believe that was Mrs. McCradle," George said. "She claims her barn is on fire or is *about* to be on fire. I could hardly understand her, she was so excited. Said it was struck by lightning. Wants the fire truck sent right out. Said her husband's gone this morning."

While George radioed the fire department, Uncle Bill began getting ready to leave with the other deputies.

"All the bridges are out," he said, looking serious. The deputies hurried. Everyone, except John and George, was out the front door within a minute of the call.

"They'll never make it on time with the bridges out," George said. "Too bad. I've known Homer and Lucy all my life. She was my teacher in first grade. One day I did a really bad . . ."

George stopped. John was gone. The young deputy rolled to the window and saw the boy running through the rain down the street. George rolled himself back over to the radio. He looked down at the chess game and shook his head.

"Good thing," he grunted. "He would have had me in three moves."

John realized he had left his coat in the police station when he was three blocks away, but he didn't slow down. He ran straight to his house, opened the garage door and pushed out the Spirit Flyer. He jumped on the old red bicycle and began speeding toward Crofts Road and the river.

By the time he got to Crofts Road he could just see the fire engine and police car racing south toward the Unionville Bridge, the red lights flashing. John blinked several times, trying to keep the rain out of his eyes. He was already soaked to his skin. He approached the dump road bridge, at least what was left of it, at his fastest speed, the balloon tires singing as they sloshed over the wet road.

John looked both ways to see if anyone was watching and then pushed down on the handlebars. He felt a chill pass through his body as the Spirit Flyer lifted off the ground. The ugly brown river churned beneath him, then was gone. John aimed the bike so it would pass over the first row of trees. He soared upward, clearing them by ten feet.

He hummed over the tops of the trees. He didn't know exactly where McCradles' farm was, but he knew the general location. He aimed the bike higher and higher, searching the land below him until he spotted it. Far off to his left, a thin column of black smoke trickled into the rain-soaked sky. John turned the bike and began pedaling faster.

Without much effort, the boy whizzed through the rainy air. When he pedaled faster, he wasn't prepared for the way the old red bike jumped forward. He thought he must be going a hundred miles an hour. But for some reason, the rain hardly touched him. He felt cold, but it was as if an invisible shield were protecting him from the wind and rain. John looked up and the clouds seemed as near as his bedroom ceiling. With a little more effort, he thought, he could go right through the clouds. But then he wouldn't be able to see McCradles' farm.

John aimed the bike lower as he approached the farm. He was just about to slow the Spirit Flyer down when a roaring flash of red-white light blinded him. At the same instant the bike seemed to be almost yanked away from him. He screamed. His eyes were open but he couldn't see, like when someone takes a picture and the flash blinds you. Only this was worse.

John could feel the Spirit Flyer beneath him, and his hands gripped the handlebars so hard they hurt. A second later his eyes adjusted and he could see again. He looked down. The bike was ok, and he wasn't hurt. He had fallen closer to the tree tops, but not dangerously close. He looked behind him. Another brilliant crack of lightning split the sky with a horrible roar. So that's what it was! The lightning had just missed him. Why had the Spirit Flyer moved so suddenly without his turning it? It was as if it had jumped out of the way of the lightning on purpose.

John aimed the bike lower and increased his speed, hoping to avoid any more close calls with lightning. Behind him, hidden in the gray clouds, a darker funnel shape moved in the mists. Two giant red eyes stared out at the flying bicycle. But John didn't see any of this; he aimed the Spirit Flyer toward the McCradle farm. A large tree next to the barn was burning furiously, but John couldn't tell if the barn was on fire. He saw the tiny figure of old Mrs. McCradle on the ground next to the tree.

John guided the old red bike down close to the road that led into the McCradle farm. He didn't want to scare Mrs. McCradle by landing on her front lawn. Instead, he leveled the Spirit Flyer off at about a foot above the road, then flew all the way to her rock driveway.

Mrs. McCradle was too busy squirting a skinny garden hose at the burning tree to notice John's arrival. He hopped off, parked his bicycle next to the house and ran over to the elderly woman.

"There're animals in the barn!" she yelled. "The door's locked. And I can't get the pump started."

The water from the hose wasn't reaching the fire in the tree branches. Inside the barn, a horse screamed, kicking its stall; chickens squawled and lambs were bleating. The fire crackled in the branches; the heat felt as if it was burning his face.

"Start the pump!" the old woman yelled, pointing at a large machine twenty feet from the barn. John ran over to the pump. At first he didn't know what to do until he realized the pump engine was just like his uncle's lawn mower engine, only bigger. John grabbed the rope and pulled. The engine sputtered, then died. He pushed the gas lever to the choke position. He grabbed the rope and pulled so hard his arm hurt. This time the pump sputtered, then coughed into life. He adjusted the gas lever, then ran back to Mrs. McCradle. Water was gushing so hard from the hose that she had trouble aiming it at the fire. She handed John the hose.

John drenched the barn roof nearest the burning branches first, hoping it wouldn't catch fire. Then he aimed the heavy stream of water at the blaze. For five minutes he wasn't sure if he could stop the fire or not. A burning branch fell on the roof of the barn. John aimed the water at the fallen branch. The animals inside the barn cried in a frenzy as the hot smoke drifted down. John kept showering the branch until it came to a wet sizzle. Then he aimed the water back onto the tree. The fire grew smaller and smaller. Soon it was no bigger than the fire his uncle grilled hamburgers on, then nothing but smoldering wet blackness.

Mrs. McCradle came running across the lawn, surprisingly fast for an older woman, holding up a key.

"I found it, I found it," she cried, running toward the barn door. As she fitted the key into the padlock on the door, John heard the sirens of the approaching fire engine and police car.

Mrs. McCradle was leading a frightened old mare out of the barn when the fire engine pulled to a halt, the men jumping off, dragging big hoses toward the still smoldering tree.

"I think it's out," she called to the men, tying the horse to her picket fence.

"What happened?" asked Sheriff Kramar as the firemen poured water on the black branches. "I didn't think we'd have a chance with the bridges out."

"Why this young man here . . ."

Mrs. McCradle looked around. John was gone. She turned in a complete circle as Sheriff Kramar looked at her uncertainly.

"Why, he was here, just a minute ago, Bill," she said. "A young man that looked just like your nephew. Just like him, though I was excited. I couldn't start the pump and he started it. Had the fire out by the time I finally found the key to the barn. Homer left it in his overalls this morning. Now where did that boy get to?"

Sheriff Kramar looked as puzzled as the old woman. He shrugged his shoulders.

"Hey, look!" one of the firemen yelled, pointing above the field behind the barn.

"What?" asked Sheriff Kramar, looking where the fireman pointed.

"I just saw something disappear into those clouds, only it wasn't a plane, too small," said the fireman. "And it was too big for a bird."

Sheriff Kramar shook his head. Mrs. McCradle disappeared into the barn to make sure the other animals were all right. The fireman kept staring at the clouds.

"Looks like we're finished here," Sheriff Kramar said. He helped the firemen put their hose away.

Then he noticed the stillness of the air. "Hey! The rain has finally stopped."

When John heard the siren, he knew he'd have to explain how he had gotten to the McCradle farm before the fire engine. While Mrs. McCradle was opening the barn door, John ran over to the Spirit Flyer parked next to her house. He waited until she was inside the barn before hopping on the old bike. He pedaled around to the back of the house and found a muddy road along the side of the field. He pointed the Spirit Flyer up and left the ground, but he leveled off at a foot above the road. He looked back, then took off, pedaling fast. The ground became a brown blur. When he approached the line of trees at the end of the field, he pointed the old bike almost straight up. The Spirit Flyer climbed like a rocket, up over the trees, heading for the clouds.

John looked back and saw the fire engine and police car parked at the farm. A group of people stood in the yard. Afraid they would see him, John pedaled faster and shot into the clouds.

Everything was misty gray and cold. John felt a little scared because he couldn't see much. But at the speed he was going, the grayness lightened and John burst through into the brilliant blue sky above the clouds, the sunlight so bright it hurt his eyes.

The clouds were white and fluffy on top, reflecting the sunlight. John leveled the Spirit Flyer, then dipped back down so the tires just touched the tops of the clouds as he sped toward Centerville. He felt light and wonderful in the brilliant sky. Out of the rain and in the sunshine, his clothes started to dry and he felt warm, as if it were a lazy summer day.

Then out of nowhere, up ahead of him far away, a swirling black shape arose out of the clouds. John braked the Spirit Flyer to a halt. In the warm silence with the white, fluffy clouds below his feet like a floor, he stared at the dark shape. He was fascinated, yet scared. He had never seen a tornado before but he figured he could race away if it got too close. John was considering flying closer to the black cloud when he froze—a cold fear suddenly raced in his blood.

The black cloud seemed to turn and take an oddly familiar shape. Then John saw the hard red eyes and the white circled X on the throat. The cloud wasn't a cloud at all, but a monstrous snake! And the cruel red eyes seemed to be staring straight at John. The snake reared higher out of the clouds. John's mouth dropped open. The snake was bigger than any building he had ever seen, and part of it was still hidden in the clouds. John almost jumped off the Spirit Flyer to run away. He lifted one foot off the pedal and began to stand. Then he realized what a long fall it was. He quickly sat back on the seat and began pedaling, aiming the bike down.

The bike dropped quickly but not before the snake opened its mouth. Just before John's head disappeared into the clouds, he saw the long red tongue lash out at him. It didn't stop but flashed straight at his head.

He saw a brilliant streak of light and shuddered in the clap of thunder that followed.

John began to pedal like crazy, trying to get through the clouds. Another loud, roaring flash of light streaked past him; the air smelled as if it were on fire. He pedaled faster, feeling like a target sitting in the sky.

He burst through the clouds and felt relieved to see the land. He dove straight down, leveling off just above the tops of the trees. As he sped along over the trees, he searched for a sheltered place to hide. He barely recognized the dump because he was moving so fast. He quickly dipped down until he was just above the old dump road. John slowed the old red bike down and rode along just off the ground. When he saw a large oak tree whose branches covered the road, he stopped. For the first time since he had left the clouds, he dared to look back. He searched the sky but saw nothing. That's when he noticed that the rain had finally stopped. And far off to the south a patch of blue sky was clearing a hole in the clouds. Maybe the rain was going away.

The sight of the blue sky made John feel better, yet he kept staring at the sky, looking for the black shape of the *thing* he had seen. He wondered if he had just imagined the snake. After all, it had been far away and the sky was so bright. But the red eyes and tongue and the white circled X on its throat had seemed real. John shivered when he thought of it.

Knowing he had to get home before his uncle did, John began pedaling the Spirit Flyer down the old dump road. He reached the flooded river quickly and flew across, landing gently on Crofts Road. No one was in sight, so John raised the old red bike a few inches off the ground and sped into town, touching down when he saw a car coming.

Unknown to John, someone had seen him speeding along Crofts Road. From his upstairs window, Barry Smedlowe watched with amazement at the speed John Kramar rode that old red junk heap of a bicycle.

And he wasn't even pedaling hard. A line of worry crossed Barry's fore-head. Something wasn't right. He couldn't see that John's tires were off the ground because John was too far away. Something strange was going on, Barry thought to himself, and he was determined to find out what.

John pedaled home, not realizing he had been seen. He parked the Spirit Flyer in its usual place and then inspected it for rust. Knowing the rain or the lightning might have hurt it, the boy checked everywhere. Just to be certain, he rubbed the bike down with a soft cotton rag and applied a thin coat of grease to the chain to keep rust away. Satisfied the old red bike was ok, John quickly changed clothes, then ran down to the police station to continue the chess game with George.

Fifteen minutes later his uncle arrived with the other deputies. Uncle Bill looked at John strangely. John tried to think of something to say, but then a phone call came for Sheriff Kramar. John looked back at the chessboard. The kings and the queens confused him. John made a bad move and George looked up at him.

"Sure you want to go there?"

"What?" John asked, looking over at his uncle still talking on the phone.

"You sure that's the move you want?"

"Yeah," John said. George sighed, then moved his queen.

"Checkmate," he said. He rolled his wheelchair over to the file cab-inet.

John looked down at the board and realized what a dumb mistake he had made. Sheriff Kramar was still talking, his back turned. John saw his chance and quietly left the station.

Later that night around the supper table, Uncle Bill was telling his family about the fire at the McCradle farm.

". . . And the odd thing was that she claimed that this mystery boy, who appeared out of nowhere, started the pump for her and put out the fire. But we didn't see this boy anywhere. And he couldn't have left by the road. But what's even stranger is that she claimed this boy looked like John."

The whole family looked at John. He said nothing, but shrugged his shoulders and smiled.

"I guess she got confused, worrying about the fire and her animals," Uncle Bill said. The rest of the family nodded sympathetically. Everyone knew the McCradles and liked them. John's arm hurt as he passed the mashed potatoes to Susan. As he rubbed the sore place on his arm, he remembered how hard he had pulled the rope on the pump.

After the children had gone to bed, Mr. and Mrs. Kramar sat in the kitchen drinking hot cocoa. Mrs. Kramar rubbed her husband's neck.

"You know that Lucy McCradle isn't any more confused in the head than I am." Mr. Kramar said, staring off into space. "I'm going back out there tomorrow and look around. There ought to be tracks or something."

"There must be a logical explanation," Mrs. Kramar replied. "There's always . . ."

"No, there isn't," he interrupted. "There isn't *always* a logical explanation. Like funnel clouds all around Centerville, and a rain that lasts nine days while towns nearby don't get a drop. What's logical about that? It's just too much like . . . like before."

"I don't think there's any connection," she said, though in her heart she shared the same fear.

"Well, I'm going back out to her farm tomorrow and take her a picture of John. If he hadn't been with George the whole time playing chess, I would know for . . ." Mr. Kramar stopped, lost in thought for a moment. "You know, I need to ask George some questions tomorrow too."

"At least the rain has stopped," Mrs. Kramar said. "That's a good sign."

"Maybe so," Mr. Kramar sighed. "Maybe so."

GROUNDED
AGAIN
· · · · · · · · ·
6

Horace Grinsby's red phone was glowing off and on, not ringing. He put his cup of coffee on the dashboard of the black truck and picked up the phone.

"Yessir?" he said, then listened. A frown crossed his face. "That's too bad. But of course we know who has it now for sure. That's some help."

Grinsby listened again. A slow smile spread across his face.

"Splendid idea," he gushed. "Splendid idea."

Then Grinsby listened for a long time. He chuckled.

"Right away, sir," he said. "Right away."

Grinsby hung up and the red phone stopped glowing. He chuckled once more and finished his coffee. From the back of the truck he got a cardboard box. He opened the box to make sure everything was there, then stepped outside. He locked the doors, then whistled all the way to the sheriff's office.

John and Roger had just parked their bicycles in front of the sheriff's office. Down the street they saw an odd man with a black derby and black suit walking toward them. The man was whistling and carrying a cardboard box. Although he seemed fairly old, it was hard to tell; he ran up the sheriff's office steps. At the top he stopped and stared down at the Spirit Flyer, rubbing his lip.

"Is one of you the owner of this bicycle?" Grinsby asked, pointing at the Spirit Flyer.

"I am," John said.

"And who might you be?"

"John Kramar."

"Ah," Grinsby said, smiling. "The son of the sheriff?"

"Well, sort of," John mumbled. He didn't like explaining that his parents had died. "He's my uncle."

"I see, I see," Grinsby said. "Well, I am Horace Grinsby of Goliath Toys. No doubt you boys have heard of the bicycle contests and race my company is sponsoring in this fair town of . . . of Centerville."

"Yeah!" both boys said at once.

"I'm just dropping off entry forms and bicycle safety booklets," Grinsby said. "I'm sure you'll each want one."

John and Roger followed Grinsby inside. George was at the radio table as usual, and Sheriff Kramar was behind his desk. He stood up when he saw Grinsby and the boys come into the office.

"I have the entry forms and bicycle safety books, Sheriff, as you requested," Grinsby said, putting the box on the long counter in the office. "And the first two entry forms go to these two young men, John and . . . uh . . ."

"I'm Roger."

"Yes, Roger," Grinsby said. He gave an entry form to each boy.

"What about the bicycle safety books?" Roger asked.

"Certainly," Grinsby replied. He pulled out two thin booklets, gave one to Roger and started to give one to John. When he paused, a frown crossed his face. Without saying a word he put the safety booklet back in the box.

"Can't I have one?" John asked.

"May I have a word with you privately, Sheriff?" Grinsby said. Sheriff Kramar looked puzzled, but nodded, opening the door to the back office. The two men went inside and closed the door.

"What was that about?" John asked George. "Why didn't he give me a book?"

"Beats me," George said, scratching his head. He looked at John. "By the way, where did you run off to Saturday morning? I never thought to ask you."

"Well, I . . . uh, went home," John said. He suddenly felt afraid. He didn't want to lie, yet he didn't want to explain about the Spirit Flyer. Not yet. He hoped the fire at McCradles' farm had been forgotten.

The young deputy stared hard at John. John looked down at his sneakers.

"Your uncle was asking me about what happened to you after we got that call from Mrs. McCradle. I almost forgot you ran off, what with Mrs. McCradle screaming on the telephone, hollering about her barn."

John shifted uneasily on his feet. He didn't like the way George kept looking at him.

"So you ran home," George said. "Did you go anywhere after that?"

John's mouth was suddenly dry. He coughed, trying to think of something he could say without lying, yet not saying he had flown to McCradles' farm. Luckily, the office door slammed. John had never been so happy to see Barry Smedlowe and three of the Cobra Club members, Doug, Robert and Scott.

"I knew you were in here," Barry said. "I saw that dump—I mean, your bicycle out front. By the way, it fell over."

"I wonder how that happened," John said, giving Barry a steely look. "It was ok when I came in here. And it better be ok when I leave."

"How could his bicycle have fallen over?" Barry asked his three gang friends. They all shook their heads, but each one had the same stupid smile on his face, just like Barry. The bigger boy looked back at John. "We don't know. Maybe your training wheels fell off."

John curled his hands into fists. The dumb grin on Barry's face made him furious. Training wheels. John was about to say something, but his uncle and Grinsby came out of the office. His uncle looked unhappy.

"We'd like some entry forms and bicycle safety booklets, Sheriff Kramar, sir," Barry said in such a phony, polite voice that John wanted to laugh.

"Certainly, young man," Grinsby said, reaching into the box.

"I need to talk to you, John," his uncle said. The unhappy look had not left his face. John froze. He felt sure his uncle was going to question him about where he had been on Saturday during the time of the fire.

"I'm afraid you won't be allowed to enter the Bicycle Safety Contest," his uncle said. John's mouth dropped open.

"Why?"

"Well, I'm acting as the Judge, and as Mr. Grinsby pointed out to me, quite properly, it might look bad if I'm judging you since you're in my family. It's called conflict of interest. You can enter the Best-Looking Bicycle Contest and the race but not the Safety Contest. We don't want people to think I was unfair as a Judge. I'm sorry, but that's the way it is. Rules are rules, and we need to be fair."

No one said anything for a moment. Roger looked down at the floor. John kept looking at his uncle. He couldn't believe it. He had been counting on being able to do well in the Safety Contest because he knew he would have trouble in the race. He knew for sure he didn't have a chance in the Best-Looking Bicycle Contest.

"What tough luck," Barry Smedlowe said. "You win some, you lose some, John old pal. Let's go, guys."

The boys left, slamming the door. But Barry's awful, braying laugh and the hoots of the other Cobra Club members carried through the door.

"Extremely sorry, young man," Grinsby said, tipping his hat. He smiled at everyone in the room, then left.

John looked back to his uncle. He felt the tears creeping into his eyes.

"I'm sorry, John, but as sheriff I have responsibilities," Uncle Bill said. "When I agreed to judge this contest, I didn't even think about its interfering with you. I don't like to break my commitments. I think I could judge fairly, but it might look bad to other people. Rules are rules. And in cases like this, families are usually prohibited from . . ."

"Sure, rules are rules," John said bitterly. "Rules are always rules."

Then, afraid he might cry, John turned and ran out of the sheriff's office. He almost knocked Grinsby down the steps as he picked up the Spirit Flyer. John jumped on and pedaled away as fast as he could. Grinsby, who had been examining though not touching the Spirit Flyer, began to chuckle as he watched John ride away. "Splendid idea," he said softly. "Soon he will make that trash-heap bike ineffective. Splendid idea." He began laughing louder.

John raced around Centerville not caring where he was going. He didn't stop at stop signs and almost got hit by cars twice. He yelled at the cars and kept pedaling fast. All he could think of was how unfair everything was. I ought to just fly away and never come back to this crummy little town, he thought. Rules are rules, hah! Who cares?

John pedaled out to Crofts Road, racing toward the river and washed-out bridge. At the last minute he pointed the bicycle up and the Spirit Flyer left the ground. Maybe I'll never come back, he thought.

Although John was angry, he knew in his heart that running away wouldn't solve his problem. But he was too angry to notice that the Spirit Flyer wasn't working like before. Although the old red bike was flying, it had left the ground much slower than it usually did. And it didn't go nearly as fast. John barely flew high enough to go over the trees across the river, but he didn't notice; all he could think of was how unfair his uncle was.

John flew over the tops of the trees, not watching where he was going. He wanted the freedom of the air. He pedaled furiously, but the old red bike plodded through the air like a sick blimp. As John began sweating, he suddenly realized the bike wasn't acting normal.

"Fly, you stupid bike, fly!" John said, shaking the handlebars. But the Spirit Flyer went slower even though he pedaled harder. John pointed the handlebars up, but the bike wouldn't rise. He pedaled faster. The old bike continued plodding along. John started to yell at the old bike and kick the front tire. Just then he saw a small figure riding on Crofts Road.

John stared at the person and realized it was Barry Smedlowe. A wonderfully ugly thought came into John's mind as he saw Barry far below; now was the time for revenge!

John circled in the air so he was behind Barry. Since the Spirit Flyer didn't make any noise, Barry was unaware of the flying bicycle high above him.

John checked his pockets to see if he had anything he could drop like a bomb on Barry. His pockets were empty. Then John had a horribly perfect idea; he would swoop down, dive-bombing toward Barry, and when he was almost there, he would scream "Chickeeeen!" and scare Barry half to death. At the same moment he might even spit, then pull the bicycle back up and fly away. Barry would think he had been attacked by a flying saucer. John smiled, thinking how scared the mighty president of the Cobra Club would be. It's just what he deserves, John thought, as he stopped in the air above Barry.

When John felt ready, he pointed the Spirit Flyer down, aiming straight at the unsuspecting bully. As the old red bike shot toward the ground, John pedaled as hard as he could and worked up a wad of spit in his mouth. Barry continued riding along the road not hearing or seeing a thing.

The Spirit Flyer was only twenty feet away when it happened. Just as John was about to spit, then scream chicken, the old red bike suddenly lost power. With a slight hissing sound, like water dripping onto a hot skillet, the bike slowed to a stop and dropped gently to the road, ten feet behind Barry.

John didn't know what had happened. Barry still hadn't seen him, so John pushed on the handlebars and pedaled, hoping to take the bicycle up for another try. The handlebars moved, but the old red bike stayed on the ground. John tried again. Nothing happened. John was pushing on the handlebars when Barry turned around.

"Where did you come from?" Barry asked. He looked at John strangely, since he hadn't heard anyone coming. He thought John was acting funny also, pushing up and down on that old bike's handlebars. "How did you get here?"

"How do you think?" John asked, pushing down on the handlebars once more, hoping to show Barry what the Spirit Flyer really could do. But the old red bike acted just like any other old red bike. Nothing happened. John became more frustrated than ever.

"Why do you keep bending the handlebars?" Barry demanded.

"Why do you keep asking questions?" John replied. "Leave me alone."

"You're just mad because you can't enter the Safety Contest," Barry grumbled. "Want to race back to town? You might as well get used to losing, so you won't be surprised on the day of the race."

Barry roared out his braying laugh. John was furious. Without thinking, he aimed the Spirit Flyer straight at Barry and charged.

Barry's eyes froze in wide circles. He didn't have time to move. John stood up on the pedals to get the most speed. Suddenly, he heard the same hissing noise that he had heard when he dive-bombed, right before the bike lost power. John almost fell over the handlebars as the back wheel began skidding. The brake was on, but John wasn't pushing it. The old bike was stopping itself! John held on tight as the Spirit Flyer swerved, leaving a long black skid mark over the highway. The bike stopped inches away from Barry.

Barry saw his chance and pushed his bicycle away. He raced for town. Even though he had been saved, he saw that John wasn't pushing the brake, and the strange behavior of the old red bicycle scared him.

As Barry sped away, John regained his balance. He knew the bike had stopped deliberately. He hopped off, knocked the kickstand down, then screamed at the bike.

"Why, why, why?" he yelled. The bike just leaned on its kickstand in the middle of the road. The silence infuriated John. In anger, he kicked the old bicycle, hitting it just below the seat. John screamed again, but this time from pain in his toe. The old red bicycle did not move when he kicked it.

As John hopped around on one foot, holding his toe, he heard a hot, bubbling sound and smelled something awful, a dead smell. He looked down. On the road where he had skidded to a stop, the skid mark was smoking and gurgling as if on fire. John jumped back. The skid mark was boiling and smoking like hot tar; it almost seemed to be moving, wriggling back and forth as if it were alive. John rubbed his eyes and looked closer. The skid mark *was* moving! Through the smoke he saw two red beady eyes and a red flicking tongue. John rubbed his eyes again, and when he looked the second time, the skid mark had turned completely into a snake!

Very smoothly, the snake began sliding toward John, its red tongue flicking the air. John was too surprised to run. As the snake slid closer, it opened its mouth wide, baring two long red fangs. Smoke poured out of the mouth. John coughed at the awful smell. He felt suffocated; he wanted to run but his legs felt paralyzed.

The snake stopped a foot away and then slowly rose in the air like a cobra ready to strike. A long hiss poured out of its mouth with the smoke. John stared into the awful, hypnotic eyes. The snake rose to its full height, rearing back to strike. Suddenly, the Spirit Flyer rolled across the road and stopped between John and the serpent. At that instant, the snake struck, sinking its long red fangs into the rear tire of the Spirit Flyer. The tire let out a shriek like the sound of a boiling teakettle as it slowly went flat. The black, smoking snake then slid across the road and disappeared into the tall weeds, leaving a trail of stinking smoke lingering in the air.

John finally caught his breath, though his heart was still pounding like a freight train. If he hadn't seen it so close with his own eyes, he wouldn't have believed it. He rubbed his eyes once more, then looked at the Spirit Flyer. The rear tire was totally flat. John bent down to check the puncture holes. Two globs of black sticky tarlike stuff were on the tire. He was afraid to touch it.

The skid mark on the road was gone, as if it had been erased. John coughed again. The horrible dead smell still lingered in the air.

The boy walked very carefully to the side of the road where the snake had disappeared. Though he couldn't see anything but weeds, the awful smell was stronger as if the snake was hiding nearby. John backed away.

Shaking his head, he grasped the handlebars of the Spirit Flyer and began pushing it back toward town.

THE OFFER
OF A
TRADE
· · · · · · · · ·

7

Nothing makes any sense anymore, John thought as he pushed the old red bike. He looked back, feeling he was being watched. But each time he looked, he saw nothing unusual, only the road, the weeds and pieces of trash.

The old bike seemed extra heavy because the day was hot. John was angry all over again at his uncle, at Barry, at Horace Grinsby and especially at the Spirit Flyer. He felt as if the old red bike had betrayed him by not flying. At the same time, he felt he should be thankful to the Spirit Flyer because it saved him from the snake.

John didn't know what to think. Nothing made sense. How could a bicycle fly? How could a skid mark turn into a snake? How could a tornado turn into a snake? And what about the time when the Spirit Flyer jumped out of the way of the lightning? Why did the bike stop flying and make him look like an idiot in front of Barry? John got angrier.

"Stupid bike," John muttered as he pushed. He looked back again. He thought he saw something move in the weeds. John stopped pushing and stared, searching for two red eyes or the black head of the snake.

The snake scared John but not just because it appeared from a skid mark. Though the skid mark snake didn't have the white circled X on its chest, it somehow seemed related to the snake in the dump and the tornado snake. And that's what scared John. It was bad enough to see a snake as big as a tornado or a snake made out of a skid mark. But something *deeper* scared him, as if he were trying to remember a bad dream and couldn't—a dream about the snakes. The feeling made him uneasy, as if he were being watched, even in his dreams.

Besides his fear, he felt disappointed. The bike wouldn't work. I won't be flying to the finish on this old junk-heap bike, John thought bitterly as he pushed the Spirit Flyer into the garage. John turned the bike upside-down and began to work on the flat tire. He found a rag and wiped away the black sticky substance that the snake bite had left. Then he took off the wheel. Even though he was in a bad mood, he was careful as he removed the inner tube. He didn't have enough money to buy a new one.

John pumped up the inner tube to find the holes. He figured there would be two from the snake's fangs. But when he sank the tube into a tub of water, there were no bubbles. He checked everywhere; the tube was fine.

John sighed at yet another puzzle and put the inner tube and tire back on. After he inflated the tire to the correct air pressure, he rode the old red bike out into the street for a test run. He only went a block before pushing down on the handlebars. As he expected, nothing happened. The Spirit Flyer continued to roll down the street like an ordinary bicycle. He rode back home and parked in the garage.

"Why don't you fly?" he shouted at the old red bike. "What have I done? It's not my fault, you stupid bike. What have you got against me?"

The old bike leaned against the wall. John almost expected it to answer him. It could certainly do other magic things by itself. Once again, John felt a surge of anger. He walked over to the old bike and kicked the wheel, bending three spokes. At that same instant, both tires made a shrill, hissing-teapot noise and slowly went flat, right before his eyes.

"I give up," John said. "I wish I'd never found you."

Even as he said the words, John knew he didn't really mean them. But angry people often say things they regret. John felt as if he should apologize. But that made him angry all over again. Why should I apologize to a bike? he thought. That's ridiculous. He stomped out of the garage, slamming the door behind him.

John barely talked at supper that night. He thought his uncle would ask him about the fire at McCradles' farm, but his uncle was also unusually quiet. All John wanted was to finish supper and go to his room. But his plans were interrupted when the doorbell rang.

Uncle Bill answered the door. John heard another man's voice, someone vaguely familiar. Then Uncle Bill called John. He left the table and was greeted by the happy face of Horace Grinsby.

"John, my boy," Grinsby said. "How very nice to see you! How very nice."

"Hi," John mumbled, shaking Grinsby's limp hand.

"I can't tell you how sad, how very sad I was today when your uncle and I made the difficult decision of disqualifying you for the Safety Contest."

"Sure," John said. I just bet you were sad, he thought.

"Therefore, in order to make up for your loss, I have a proposal for you," Grinsby grinned. "Something I'm sure will excite you."

"What?"

"One moment, please," Grinsby said. He went out the front door and returned, pushing a shiny, new ten-speed bicycle into the room. The bike was metal-flake black with lots of chrome. The seat was real leather. Somehow it looked familiar. Then John realized it was exactly like Barry Smedlowe's bike. On the front was a picture of a black cobra, rearing up with its mouth open. On the middle bar in gold letters was the name, Goliath Cobra.

"As an agent of Goliath Toys, I am authorized to give you this bicycle," Grinsby said. "This is our newest and best model. Quite costly, actually, but you have something my boss would like."

"What's that?" John asked. He couldn't think of anything he owned that was really valuable.

"Your old red bicycle," Grinsby said. "The one you found at the dump. I believe its brand name is Spirit Flyer?"

"But why would your boss want it?" John asked.

Grinsby frowned for a second, then smiled once more.

"Well, it so happens that my boss has an antique bicycle collection, and your bike, a Spirit Flyer, though not a really *good* specimen of the Spirit Flyer line, is nonetheless a Spirit Flyer," Grinsby said. "They are somewhat rare, besides being old."

Uncle Bill, who had been listening quietly, stared at Grinsby with more interest. Aunt Betty also looked puzzled.

"You've seen this type of bicycle before?" Uncle Bill asked.

"Why, yes, of course," he said. "Although they aren't too common, one sees them occasionally."

John's cousins, Susan, Katherine and Lois, came into the room. When they saw the shiny, new bicycle, they ran over to it, talking excitedly.

"What a pretty bicycle," Lois said.

"I don't know," Katherine replied. "It almost seems mean. Look at that snake. It looks like it wants to bite you."

"Yeah, it does, sort of," Lois said. Both girls stepped back.

"Nonsense, nonsense," Grinsby said, chuckling. "Children say the funniest things. Anyway, shall we take this out to the garage and get the Spirit Flyer? I can carry it in my truck."

"How did you know I found it at the dump?" John asked. Something about Grinsby made him suspicious, though John couldn't decide what it was.

"Oh, . . . some child told me, I think," Grinsby said. "One hears things, you know."

John thought for a moment. Everyone in the room was staring at him. Since the Spirit Flyer has stopped flying, maybe I should just trade it, John thought. He was still mad at the old bicycle. But the idea of trading, even for a new bicycle, seemed impossible.

"No, I don't think so," John said. He was surprised to hear Aunt Betty sigh. When John looked at her, she had her hand over her mouth. Uncle Bill looked uneasy. Why are they acting so funny? John wondered.

"You mean you don't want to trade?" Grinsby asked, as if he couldn't believe his ears. He looked angry for a moment, then smiled. "This Goliath Cobra Deluxe is worth four times the price of the Spirit Flyer. I can see you drive a hard bargain. Good business sense, boy. So, to sweeten the deal, I will throw in a little money. I know my boss would like this bicycle. How does a thousand dollars sound to you, young man? Plus the Goliath Cobra Deluxe?"

Everyone, including John, gasped as Grinsby took out his wallet and a fistful of bills.

"Here," he said, handing John the money. "One thousand dollars, and the Goliath Cobra Deluxe. Now, shall we load up the Spirit Flyer? I need to be going."

John stared at the money. It was the most he had ever held in his hand.

"You can buy lots of nice things with that much money, young man," Grinsby said. "You could even have enough left over to buy some pretty nice presents for these lovely young ladies here. Even your aunt and uncle."

Katherine and Lois jumped up and down and screamed in delight when they heard John might buy them a present. But Susan looked at John with fear in her eyes.

"We don't need presents," she said firmly, looking at Grinsby. "Don't worry about us, John."

"Now, young lady, don't be so . . ."

"No," John said suddenly. He gave the money back. "I don't want to sell."

Grinsby frowned for a long time saying nothing. Very reluctantly he put the money back in his wallet. Lois and Katherine looked sad. Susan smiled at John.

"Very well, I can see that you want to think it over," Grinsby said. "No need to be hasty. If you want to change your mind, let me know. I will be around town. I bid you folks a good night."

Ginsby tipped his hat, then pushed the black bicycle out the door. No one said anything until they heard his truck drive away.

"You must be crazy, John," Katherine said. "A thousand dollars! That would be better than Christmas!"

"Will you girls clean up the kitchen, please?" Mrs. Kramar asked.

"I get to dry," screamed Lois.

"Me too," said Katherine. "Susan has to wash."

Susan was quiet. She walked over to John and hugged him. John was surprised. She ran out of the room without saying a word.

"Will you sit down, John?" Uncle Bill asked. His voice was serious. He looked at his watch and then at Aunt Betty. John sat down. For some reason he felt relieved, as if a great weight had been lifted off his shoulders. But everything changed when he heard his uncle's next words.

"Lucy McCradle is coming over in just a few minutes," Uncle Bill said. "I went out to her farm today. She wants to thank you."

MRS. McCRADLE'S THANK YOU

· · · · · · · ·

8

The words were hardly out of his uncle's mouth before the doorbell rang. Aunt Betty answered it. Mrs. McCradle walked quickly into the room, shook hands with Uncle Bill, then spied John sitting on the couch.

"There you are," she said. "Yep, I knew it was you. I don't know how you got to my farm so fast or why you left without saying a word, but I never got a chance to thank you. Here."

John stood up. Mrs. McCradle handed him a large round cookie can.

"Hope you like chocolate chip," she said. "It's my best cookie. Homer likes butterscotch chip, but your uncle said you were partial to chocolate, so I made these. I sure did appreciate your starting that pump. So did Homer. And Princess. That's our horse. Well, I can't stay, got too many people to visit. Haven't been able to get to town with the bridges being out. Thanks again. Come out and ride Princess sometime. She's a little contrary, but basically a good horse. Good night, all. I can let myself out. Been doing it for seventy-six years now all by myself. Good night."

John stared at the cookie can in his hands, afraid to look up at his uncle.

"Anyone want a cookie?" he asked weakly.

"Yes," his uncle said. "But have a seat first. I have something to show you."

John sat back down on the couch. His aunt smiled at him but didn't speak. A moment later, Uncle Bill returned carrying two long white pieces of plaster.

"What's that?" John asked although he was afraid he knew. "These are plaster casts of tracks," Uncle Bill said. "Bicycle tracks. The same bicycle tracks as the tires on the Spirit Flyer. I made one of these out at McCradles' farm. I made the other with the Spirit Flyer. They are the same."

"Oh," John said.

"You did a very good thing, John," Aunt Betty said.

"But how did you get there?" Uncle Bill asked. "That's what we don't understand."

"You won't believe me," John whispered.

"Try me."

"I rode there on the Spirit Flyer," John said. He felt relieved to have the secret out.

"But the bridges were down," Uncle Bill protested. "You were in the office at the same time I was. We left before you. And we took the shortest route to her house."

"It flies," John said weakly, and then sighed. "Or at least it used to fly. It stopped flying today."

Uncle Bill and Aunt Betty looked at each other. John watched them carefully. His uncle swallowed, then cleared his throat.

"John, I believe you helped Mrs. McCradle put out the fire," Uncle Bill said, as if he were trying to convince himself.

"Really?" John asked. "I thought for sure you'd think I was crazy when I told you the Spirit . . ."

"But I don't believe your bicycle flies," Uncle Bill added. His face went hard and determined.

"But how else could I have gotten there?" John asked. He looked from his uncle's face to Aunt Betty's. She looked down, not meeting his gaze.

"There are laws in this world," Uncle Bill began patiently. "Moral laws, civil laws and scientific laws. As sheriff, I enforce civil laws. As a father and husband, I enforce moral laws in our home. But I don't have any control over scientific laws. Nature enforces them. It's against everything I know about science to say a bicycle can fly."

"But how did I get to Mrs. McCradle's if I didn't fly?" John protested. "Do you think I'm lying?"

"No, I don't think you're lying," Uncle Bill said slowly. "But I think you have a strong imagination. You probably thought you flew. Like we all pretend sometimes. Didn't you used to play with your toy tractors and space ships and pretend they were real tractors and space ships?"

"Yes," John admitted. "But I know . . ."

"I remember when you were younger," his uncle continued, "how you used to have me push you on the swing in the park. You used to say you were flying then. Do you remember calling that the 'Fly Swing'?"

"Yes, but . . ."

"Well, I think that you rode your bicycle over to Mrs. McCradle's farm," Uncle Bill said ignoring John's protests. "I think you knew she needed help so much that you *wanted* to fly. So you pedaled very fast through the rain and mud and got there ahead of us. You started the pump because you are a big enough boy to do that by yourself. And then you rode home. We somehow missed you along the road. Maybe you took a short cut we don't know about. Isn't that about the way it really happened?"

"No," John said. "It didn't happen like that at all. I know I pretend sometimes, but I wasn't pretending. How could I have gotten across the river if I was just pretending?"

A frown spread across Uncle Bill's face. Aunt Betty looked at her husband, waiting, just like John.

"You know how to swim," Uncle Bill said, shrugging his shoulders.

"But the water was fifteen feet high, Uncle Bill," John said. "And you know how fast the current is when it floods."

"Well, there must have been a drop in the river for a while," Uncle Bill said. "Flood waters drop. You probably arrived when the waters weren't so deep and swam across."

"But how could I swim with my bicycle?" John asked.

"Look," Uncle Bill said angrily. "Let's just go out to the garage right now and we'll settle this."

Uncle Bill stomped through the house and out into the garage. Seeing that the Spirit Flyer's tires were flat, he began pumping them up. He pumped so hard that John was almost afraid.

"There," Uncle Bill said, his face red. "Let's see it fly."

"I don't think it will now," John said slowly. "I tried to tell you it stopped flying today."

"Well, that's certainly convenient," Uncle Bill said. "First you tell me it flies, then you say it doesn't."

"I don't understand it, but it stopped," John said. "It just seemed to lose power. After you told me I couldn't be in the Safety Contest, I rode out of town and it flew awhile, but then it lost its power. I couldn't make it fly anymore. It sort of has a mind of its own. I can't force it to fly. I've even seen it move by itself, with no one near it."

"What?" Uncle Bill asked, looking even more doubtful.

"Well, I know this will sound crazy, but I stopped suddenly and made a skid mark," John said weakly. "But it wasn't really a skid mark. Well, I mean it *was* a skid mark, but then it turned into this awful black snake. It smoked and hissed and was going to bite me, but the Spirit Flyer rolled between me and the snake, and it bit the Spirit Flyer's back tire. The tire went flat. But when I fixed it there weren't any holes. Then later I kicked it and both tires went flat. I was mad because it wouldn't fly."

"Oh, I see," Uncle Bill said, nodding his head. "Just like that."

"You don't believe me," John said. He wasn't surprised, but he began to feel more frustrated than ever. He didn't know which was worse, having Uncle Bill think he was a liar or think he didn't know the difference between pretending and the truth.

"I believe what I see," Uncle Bill said, "or what can be proved scientifically. Go ahead and try to make the bike fly. I'm willing to watch."

"But I don't think it will fly now," John said. He got on the Spirit Flyer without any hope. Uncle Bill opened the garage door. John pedaled out into the driveway, turning in a circle.

"Well," Uncle Bill said, his arms folded across his chest, "does it grow wings or something?"

John pushed down on the handlebars. As he expected, nothing happened; the bike just rolled forward. John tried it again, then another time. Nothing happened.

"I guess that settles that," Uncle Bill said. "You just let your imagination get carried away, that's all. Now let's go to bed."

Uncle Bill turned to go into the house. John raced to catch up with him. John felt worse when he saw Susan, Katherine and Lois watching him from the door. Aunt Betty looked sad.

"But I'm telling you it flew," John protested. "And it saved me from the black snake. Not only the one on the ground, but the big one, the one that spit lightning at me. At first I thought it was a big tornado, but it turned around and I saw it was a snake. It had red eyes and a white circled X on its throat. But the Spirit Flyer jerked me out of the way of the lightning. That snake must have spit it at me the first time too, but I didn't see it in the clouds."

At the mention of the word *tornado,* Uncle Bill froze halfway to the door. When he turned around, his face had gone pale. He looked nervously at Aunt Betty. She seemed frightened.

"What did you say about a tornado and a snake?" Uncle Bill asked. His voice cracked.

"I know you'll think I'm crazy or imagining this too," John said. "But when I flew away from McCradles' farm, I didn't want you to see me, so I flew straight up through the clouds. They are all white and fluffy on top once you get through the gray. Anyway, I saw a funnel cloud. At least I thought it was a funnel cloud, but then it turned around, and it was this *huge* black snake with red . . ."

"Stop it!" Uncle Bill shouted, putting his hands over his ears. "I don't want to hear anymore."

John felt scared. He had never seen his uncle like this.

Uncle Bill seemed afraid. Katherine, who had been watching with the rest of the girls, began to cry.

"You girls take Katherine inside, please," Aunt Betty said.

Susan, seeing the serious expression on her mother's face, quickly took Lois and Katherine by the hand and led them inside. The silence in the garage lasted a long time. John was afraid to say anything else.

"It's time for bed," Uncle Bill said softly as if he were exhausted. "Let's just forget this whole thing. I don't want to hear any more snake stories or flying bicycle stories or skid-marks-that-turn-into-snakes stories. The rain has stopped and it's probably over. We'll forget the whole thing. Let's just go to bed. I think you inherited too much imagination from your father. I'm too tired to think anymore. I've got enough worries. Flying bicycles are just not scientific. They break every law I know. We'll forget we had this crazy discussion. Good night."

Uncle Bill walked straight into the house without looking at John or Aunt Betty. John watched his uncle until he disappeared into the house.

When he looked back to Aunt Betty, he was surprised to see a tear roll down her cheek.

"I don't understand," John said. "Is Uncle Bill mad at me? Did he want me to sell the Spirit Flyer to Mr. Grinsby? I guess he thinks I'm crazy for not selling *and* because I said the Spirit Flyer flew. I don't know. I didn't really want that other bicycle. That cobra reminded me too much of the snake I saw above the clouds and the one that was wrapped around the Spirit Flyer when I found it at the dump."

"There was another snake?" Aunt Betty asked.

John told her the whole story about how he and Roger found the Spirit Flyer. Then he told her how he discovered it flew. Aunt Betty listened carefully without saying a word.

"And when I heard about the fire at Mrs. McCradle's," John continued, "I ran home and flew to her house like I said before. I don't think I imagined it. How could I have gotten across the river?"

"I don't know, John," Aunt Betty said quietly. "I don't understand a lot of things. Just like you. I know that Uncle Bill isn't really mad at you. He loves you like his own son. But he is upset."

"Why?" John asked.

"Well, because . . ." Suddenly her eyes filled with tears again. John felt more confused. "I think Uncle Bill will tell you when the time is right. Or maybe you should talk to Grandfather Kramar."

Grandfather Kramar lived on a farm about two hundred fifty miles north of Centerville. Every summer, John and Susan went to live with Grandfather and Grandmother Kramar for two or three weeks. They always had a great time helping with the chores, playing in the barn, riding the horse and swimming in the creek. There was always something interesting to do at the farm.

"Grandfather Kramar knows many things," Aunt Betty said. John waited for an explanation. His aunt looked troubled.

"What kind of things?" John asked finally.

Aunt Betty looked out into the night. She bit her lip. John had never seen such an expression on her face.

"I promised Bill that I wouldn't talk about it, John," she finally said. "I'm sorry to be so mysterious, but I made a promise. Unless he wants to tell you, or Grandfather . . ." She stopped talking, looking out into the darkness.

"But I don't understand," John said, puzzled by his aunt's words. "Do you think I'm imagining things?"

"I don't know what I think for sure," Aunt Betty said slowly. "But I know things aren't always . . . always scientific. I mean, I believe things happen that maybe science doesn't know about yet. Things you can't prove or disprove. There aren't always clear explanations for things."

"You can say that again," John said, glad to know his aunt didn't think he was crazy. "I don't know how the Spirit Flyer flew, or anything about those snakes. I just know it happened, that's all. Whether anyone believes me or not, I know what happened."

But at that same instant, John felt a surge of doubt.

"It's time for bed," Aunt Betty said. "We've had a long day. All of us."

She fluffed John's hair with her hand. After John closed the garage door, he parked the Spirit Flyer in its usual place.

"By the way," John said as they started into the house, "what did Uncle Bill mean when he said I got too much imagination from my father?"

His aunt stopped in the doorway. She stared straight ahead without saying a word.

"Did I say something wrong?" John asked.

"No, John," his aunt said. "It's just that . . . well, brothers don't always agree about things. But Bill misses your father. Now let's not talk anymore. Time for bed.

And before John could ask anything else, Aunt Betty turned out the light and walked quickly into the house. John stood by the door thinking for about five minutes, then walked quietly to his room.

For a long time he couldn't sleep, but lay in the darkness, looking at the ceiling. Soon he was dreaming what he had dreamed before, but this time he remembered the dream. He was flying the Spirit Flyer high above the clouds. The black tornado snake rose up and opened its huge mouth. Without resisting, John flew the Spirit Flyer into the huge mouth, going below the two red fangs. The darkness swallowed him and he was afraid. He screamed for his father. Far off in the darkness, he thought he heard a voice answer.

THE COBRA
CLUB
STRIKES
· · · · · · · · ·

9

The last days of school dragged to an end. Like everyone else, John was impatient for summer. But unlike his classmates and friends, John wasn't excited about the bicycle contests and race. Each day after school the streets of Centerville were crowded with bicycles: big bikes, little bikes, ten-speeds and dirt bikes. Every eligible girl and boy was practicing safety rules or getting in shape for the race or fixing up a bike for the Best-Looking Contest. Every bike in town was being ridden, every bike except the Spirit Flyer.

John stopped riding the Spirit Flyer four days after the night he told his uncle and aunt it could fly. He tried several times to make the old red bike fly, but each time he failed. And each time he failed he became more discouraged. He gave up all hope that the Spirit Flyer would fly again. The worst thing was that his uncle would never believe his stories about it.

Uncle Bill remained strangely silent about the Spirit Flyer after that night. He never talked about the bike. He acted normal, though John got the feeling that he was *trying* to act normal. At night, more than once, John overheard his aunt and uncle whispering. His uncle sounded upset. One time his uncle said, "It's over. We don't have to worry. It's over."

John figured it was over too, that the Spirit Flyer would never fly again. He began wondering if it had ever really flown. In his heart he knew that it had. Yet why did it stop flying especially when he needed to prove his story to Uncle Bill? John felt betrayed.

John seriously reconsidered Horace Grinsby's offer to buy the Spirit Flyer. He didn't like the Goliath Cobra, but it was a ten-speed. And a thousand dollars was a mountain of money.

John figured he could sell the Goliath Cobra and have even more money. He could buy the kind of bike he wanted. Maybe one just like his old ten-speed. If I sold the Spirit Flyer today, John thought, I'd still have time to practice for the race. I could even enter the Best-Looking Contest.

John visited all the stores that sold bicycles. He looked carefully at each model and each brand. He sat on the ones he liked. John checked and compared prices. He thought of what he could buy with the leftover money. As the day of the race and contests came closer, John felt he should sell the Spirit Flyer and forget it. What was so special about a fat, ugly old bike? It didn't fly anymore. I might as well sell it, John thought.

But John just couldn't bring himself to do it. Although he was angry at the old bike, deep inside he didn't want to get rid of it. In his heart, he hoped the Spirit Flyer would fly again.

Finally the last day of school arrived. After the awards assembly and the class parties that Thursday morning, all the students cheered at the final bell. And after school most children went to parties at their friends' houses.

To celebrate the beginning of summer vacation, Barry Smedlowe called a special meeting of the Cobra Club. For regular meetings, the boys met at Barry's house. But for secret Cobra Strike meetings, the club met in an abandoned shed behind the hardware store. That day they were meeting secretly in the shed. Barry closed the door and got right down to business.

"We all know the trouble John Kramar has caused us in the past, calling us names and making fun of us," Barry said. "I say we carry out a Cobra Strike against this enemy of the club."

The other boys laughed and nodded. A Cobra Strike was their term for revenge or some other secret action that might get them in trouble.

"I tell you, John Kramar's planning something sneaky," Barry said. "I've been noticing that he isn't practicing on that old dump-heap bicycle. He must have some secret plan to win the race tomorrow. Maybe he's practicing so we don't see him. I say we fix it so he doesn't enter the race."

"How?" Doug Barns asked. He was usually afraid of Barry's ideas for Cobra Strikes. He thought Barry went too far, like the time they spray-painted bad words on the school cafeteria walls. Yet Doug knew he couldn't quit the Cobra Club. The punishment was terrible. It was part of the rules. No one had quit.

"I have a plan," Barry said, then laughed his horrible laugh. "Near the corner of Main Street and Elm there's a big hole in the road where they've been fixing the sewer. The flood messed it up. My plan is that John Kramar has a little accident. And maybe he'll fall into that hole when he has his accident."

"Are you crazy?" Doug asked. "That hole's six feet deep and full of water. He could drown!"

"Who's president here?" Barry asked, looking coldly at Doug. "You want to quit, chicken?"

"No," Doug said. "It's just that . . ."

"Don't be a scaredy cat," Barry said. "He wont drown. Besides, it won't be our fault. Listen, this is what we'll do."

Barry began to whisper. The other boys smiled as the bigger boy told them his plan. Then they rushed out of the abandoned shed, ready for action.

John was staring out the window, thinking about the Spirit Flyer and the next day's race, when he saw Susan run across the yard, her hair and clothes soaking wet. At first John wanted to laugh, but then he saw that she was crying. John met her at the door. Her eyes were very red.

"What happened?" John asked.

"I was coming home from Barbara's and they attacked me!" Susan blurted out.

"Who?"

"I don't know," Susan said. "All of sudden a water balloon hit me right in the face. Someone yelled something like, 'Strike.' Then I could barely move, they threw so many balloons. And they have something in them that stings your eyes, like soap. It really hurts."

"Where were they?" John asked.

"Down by Main Street and Elm," Susan said. "I better change. I'm dripping all over the rug."

John felt a surge of anger. Like a warm fire, it began in his stomach, then spread up through his shoulders and arms, and finally into his hands which became fists. He knew it was the Cobra Club the instant Susan said the word *strike*. Attacking someone who wasn't looking sounded just like them, especially Barry Smedlowe.

John ran to the garage. He jerked open the door, then hopped on the Spirit Flyer as he pushed it down the driveway. He didn't care whether it flew or not; it wasn't far to Elm and Main. He wanted to get there before the Cobra Club got away. Little did he realize they were waiting especially for him.

John was pedaling so furiously that he didn't even see Roger pedal around the corner. Roger followed, sensing that something was wrong. But John didn't notice.

"Just don't fail me now," John whispered to the old red bike as he raced along the street. "I'm sorry I was mad at you. I don't care if you don't fly and I don't understand. Just get me there without falling apart."

John rounded the corner and saw him. Down at the end of the street, Barry Smedlowe sat on his bicycle. He had something in his hands, but John couldn't see it clearly. He assumed it was water balloons. What John couldn't see was the large hole right in front of Barry.

"Here he comes," Barry said. The Cobra Club had removed the yellow light and the sign that said, "WARNING: KEEP AWAY." The other boys were hiding behind parked cars, their hands full of water balloons with dishwashing detergent inside. "When I say 'Strike,' let him have it."

John pedaled faster when he saw Barry. Roger, using the lower gears on his ten-speed, gained on his best friend. Roger knew something was wrong, but he couldn't quite put his finger on it. Then he remembered the hole. Surely he will see the hole, Roger thought.

At that moment, an old pickup truck rounded the corner and accelerated down Elm Street. John didn't notice the truck but looked straight at Barry. The president of the Cobra Club laughed, then raised his right arm.

"Strike!" Barry yelled, throwing the balloon. At that same instant, John noticed the huge hole right in front of him. John stomped back on the brake and jerked to the left, trying to avoid the hole, when six water balloons hit him. Four got him in the head, two in the chest. The detergent stung his eyes. John hit the brake harder because he couldn't see where he was going. He thought he was going to miss the hole. But what he couldn't see was the pickup truck coming from the opposite direction.

Roger screamed. Barry's face turned pale. He hadn't wanted to hurt John badly. Old man Turner wasn't paying attention as he drove along; then suddenly he saw a boy on a bicycle right in front of the truck. He hit the brake and horn, knowing it was too late.

John opened his eyes just a crack and glimpsed the shiny chrome fender of the pickup. The horn blared at him. He knew he was going to crash. Then suddenly he was lifted up, higher and higher and higher. He was sailing through the air. He saw the roof, then the back of the pickup below him. John continued beyond the truck a few feet; then the Spirit Flyer landed gently back on the street and stopped.

John was wiping his eyes, trying to get the burning soap out, when Roger and Mr. Turner ran up to him.

"Are you all right?" Roger asked. "What happened? What happened?"

John rubbed his eyes with his shirt sleeve once more. His hair and clothes were soaked and beginning to feel cold. Water dripped off his chin and elbows onto the street.

"I'm ok," John said.

"Are you sure? I didn't hear you hit my truck," Mr. Turner said. "But you must have hit it. All of a sudden you was shooting up over the cab and that's all I saw. You must have a lot of luck, boy. You sure you're ok?"

"Yeah, I'm fine. But I don't think it was luck," John said quietly, realizing that once again the Spirit Flyer had saved his life.

"He didn't even touch the truck!" Doug Barns screamed from across the road. All the Cobra Club members stood in a circle. Barry Smedlowe looked as if he had seen a ghost.

"I saw it too," Jimmy Roundhouse, another club member, said. "It looked like it jumped right over the whole thing. It never touched nothing."

"Why are you all wet, boy?" Old Mr. Turner asked John. "There's not a cloud in the sky."

John turned to point at the Cobra Club, but they had jumped on their bicycles and were pedaling as fast as they could go. John grunted, seeing the troublemakers running away.

"How did you do it?" Roger asked. "I couldn't see whether you hit or not. What happened?"

John looked at Roger and the old man. He wondered if he should tell them. He doubted that they would believe him. He had learned from Uncle Bill that people sometimes see only what they want to see. John knew the old red bike had flown over the truck. He knew it wasn't luck or an accident.

"I guess it flew over," John said. "That's what everyone saw. My eyes were closed; I didn't see much."

"Well, that was the craziest thing I've ever seen!" exclaimed Mr. Turner, scratching his head. "See you boys later. And watch out where you're going from now on."

The old man got back into his pickup and drove away. John stared at the truck's skid marks.

"That hole's dangerous," Roger said. "They meant you to fall in. They moved the sawhorses on purpose. We better put them back before someone really does fall in."

"Yeah," John agreed. He helped Roger move the sawhorses and signs back in front of the hole. John left wet footprints everywhere he walked.

"I still don't understand," Roger said, shaking his head. "I just don't understand."

"Neither do I," John said truthfully. What had made the Spirit Flyer fly again, he wondered? Would it fly if he tried to make it fly?

"I better go home and change my clothes," John said. "Maybe we can practice for the race later."

"I've got to buy some stuff for my mom," Roger said. "I was supposed to be home already. I saw you going by and tried to catch up."

"Thanks," John said, watching a puddle form around his tennis shoes. "Maybe I'll see you later."

John hopped on the Spirit Flyer. Roger waved, then rode off toward Main Street. John pedaled slowly down Elm Street, wondering if Barry or any other Cobra Club members were hiding nearby. He didn't think they would attack again, but he wasn't sure. As he rode home, he looked at each parked car carefully, almost expecting someone to jump out with a water balloon. John didn't know it, but the Cobra Club was in its secret

clubhouse arguing about how a bicycle could fly over a truck.

Another person was arguing too. Inside the black truck marked Goliath Toys, Horace Grinsby was complaining on the glowing red telephone.

"I realize very well the bike is without the instruments," Grinsby said. "It's not like I died yesterday. But I tell you I need help. I just saw the bike and boy fly over a moving truck. The stupid idiot couldn't see a thing. His eyes were full of soap. Ha, ha. My idea. I'm working with a boy here, a real candidate, sir. He has a club of little cobras. They even call themselves the Cobra Club. I thought you'd like the name. I suggested the ambush to the boy, who suggested it to the club. The Kramar boy was bombed with balloons. I had it planned perfectly right down to the exact instant the truck turned the corner. He didn't have time to move the handlebars. I say he has a strong cloud around him. He's being protected more than we thought. I need help."

Grinsby listened for a long time. He frowned. He shook his head, not speaking.

"Yes, I realize the instruments aren't attached," Grinsby said. "I know that's in our favor, but . . ."

Grinsby listened again. He continued frowning.

"If you say so, sir," Grinsby said. "Of course we always have that option. I was hoping it would be easier. I will keep you informed. I have plans to use the Cobra Club boy tonight. Shall I proceed? Maybe we can finish and leave this ugly little town."

Grinsby listened a while longer, then hung up. The phone stopped glowing. Grinsby watched John riding down the street. That brat is ruining everything, he thought. Then John was out of sight.

"Just you wait, young man," Grinsby said. "The truck was nothing. Just you wait."

BARRY'S
WILD
RIDE
· · · · · · · · ·
10

At one minute to midnight that same night, Barry Smedlowe stood in the darkness next to the black truck advertising Goliath Toys. He looked nervously in both directions. He was sure no one at his house had heard him sneak out. And he had stayed in the shadows as he ran to keep his appointment with Grinsby. He knocked on the door of the truck. Quietly the door opened. Barry climbed inside.

Horace Grinsby smiled at Barry for several seconds, then spoke.

"You failed, didn't you," Grinsby said. "But never mind. We all fail. But you must not fail tonight. Bring me the bicycle and the money will be yours. Are you ready?"

"I think so," Barry said. "But can I have some more of that candy first? That kind you gave me this afternoon?"

"Certainly, lad, certainly," Grinsby said. The candy always seemed to work, especially with greedy boys like Barry. Grinsby opened a large black sack and took out six pieces. The candies were a little larger than a marble and wrapped in black cellophane. Barry peeled the wrapper off one. The oblong candy was hard and green on the outside, tasting like a strong mint. A red slash in the center looked just like a cat's eye. The red part had a strange flavor, very, very sweet, but an unusual sweetness. Then inside was a black chewy center that looked like licorice, but it didn't taste like anything Barry had ever eaten before, a sort of bitter taste. Barry popped the candy into his mouth. He rolled it around on his tongue.

"What do you call these anyway?" Barry asked. I've never seen them for sale around here."

"Oh, they're very special candies," Grinsby said. "The company I work for makes them. You can't really buy them. We only give them to our friends and best customers. We call them Sweet Temptations."

"Can I have some more?"

"No," Grinsby said. "Not until you complete the job. You better get going."

"But what if someone sees me," Barry complained. "His uncle is the sheriff. I could get in trouble."

"That's your problem," Grinsby said. "If you want to chicken out, I can get someone else who wants the money. And the candy. So, are you ready or not?"

"I guess so," Barry said slowly. But in his heart he wasn't sure. The close call with the pickup truck had scared him. Barry still couldn't understand how John avoided the crash. The old red bike seemed to fly right over the truck. Barry thought that was the real reason why Grinsby wanted the bike. "Why do you want that old bike so much? Why don't you steal it yourself?"

"As I told you," Grinsby said, smiling broadly, "my company wants to make sure the right bike wins tomorrow's race: a Goliath Cobra. And we're not really stealing it; we're borrowing it for a while. I'll return it myself after the race with a little money attached to the seat. I offered to buy the old bike, but that silly Kramar boy wouldn't sell. This will just be a harmless joke. So it isn't really stealing, is it?"

"I guess not," Barry said. "You said you'd help me though. Are you coming with me?"

"Of course not," Grinsby said. "I'm staying right here in the truck. You bring the bike to me."

"But how will I get in?" Barry asked. "You said you'd help."

"Use this," Grinsby said. He reached into his vest pocket and pulled out a black metal object. The dark metal glinted in his palm. One end had the head of a snake, and the other end was a flattened rod with a small X on the end. "This will fit any lock at the Kramar house."

"How can it do that?" Barry asked. "I've never heard of a key like that."

"It's like a skeleton key, only more special," Grinsby grunted. "Hurry up. You haven't got all night."

Grinsby gave the unusual key to Barry. For some reason the key felt warm—not really hot, but warmer than a piece of metal should feel, Barry thought. He would have said something, but Grinsby was impatient. Barry put the key into his pocket. The truck door creaked eerily in the dark stillness of the street.

"Don't be long," Grinsby hissed.

Barry nodded, then walked quickly away from the truck. The streets were quiet and empty. Barry walked in the shadows, taking no chances of being seen. But he didn't realize that he was being watched. A large black cat with green eyes crept softly behind him, watching every step the boy took.

Barry popped another piece of candy into his mouth. He loved the sweet, minty taste the best. The red part was good, but the black part was too bitter, even making his stomach ache a bit. The strong sweet flavors almost covered the bitterness. Barry sucked greedily on the Sweet Temptation as he crept through the darkness.

When he got close to the Kramar house, he stopped. For the first time he began to feel afraid. I could really get in trouble, Barry thought. What if they catch me? Barry stared at the dark house. It seemed like a voice was telling him no, don't do it. Yet right away another voice whispered, telling him to hurry up and steal the bike. His second candy was almost gone. The strange bitter taste filled his mouth. Maybe I should just go home, he thought.

Barry popped in another Sweet Temptation. The strong sweet flavor made him feel better. It'll be easy to take the bike, Barry thought. Do it, the voice whispered. It's only borrowing, not stealing.

Barry threw the candy wrapper down and walked quickly toward the Kramar house. Hiding in the shadows, he sneaked up to the small side door to the garage. Barry touched the strange key in his pocket; it still felt unusually warm. The sweet candy taste increased in his mouth as he held the key. He didn't think the key would fit the lock, but he tried it anyway. To his surprise, the key slid right in. He heard three clicks, and the door opened a crack. I didn't even turn the key, Barry said to himself. I didn't even turn the doorknob, but it opened. Barry sucked harder on the Sweet Temptation, then stepped inside the garage.

He waited, letting his eyes get used to the darkness. Then he saw it. The Spirit Flyer was leaning against the wall next to a high metal shelf. Barry tiptoed over to the old bike, being careful not to bump anything. He grabbed the handlebars and pushed the bike to the door. He was extra careful not to make noise. Once outside, he closed the door softly, making sure it was locked. Then he wiped away his fingerprints using his shirt tail.

Barry was sure no one saw him pedal to the black truck. A large black cat did chase him for a while, but then it disappeared into the darkness. That was easy, Barry thought, laughing quietly as he rode up to the truck.

Horace Grinsby was watching through the window. What a stupid, greedy boy, he thought. He would believe anything you told him. Grinsby chuckled to himself. He put on a pair of black gloves and picked up a large hammer. His hands shook in excitement as he opened the back doors of the truck.

"I got it!" Barry said. "It was really easy. The key worked like magic."

"Yes, of course," Grinsby said. He hid the hammer behind his back. "It's a very special key. It's even better than magic. Give it back now."

Barry took the unusually warm key and put it in the black-gloved hand. He sat back on the seat of the Spirit Flyer waiting for the money and candy Grinsby had promised. But the odd man remained silent, just staring at the old bike.

"Can I have my money and candy?" Barry asked. "I need to get home."

"Certainly," Grinsby said. "But you must do one more small thing for me."

"What?" Barry asked suspiciously. He didn't like the look in Grinsby's eyes.

"Why don't we *change* the Spirit Flyer a tiny bit?" Grinsby said, then chuckled. "With this. We can still return it later, only *changed.*"

The man in the derby pulled the hammer out from behind his back. The hammer was big, like a small sledgehammer. Something wet and dark dripped from it onto the street.

"What do you mean?" Barry asked. "And what's that stuff dripping?" He reached over and touched the wetness. He held his finger in the light. It was red and looked just like . . . "Hey, what is this anyway? It looks just like blood or something."

"Don't be silly, young man," Grinsby hissed. "It's a special type of grease, that's all. Now let's not waste any more time. Hit the bike. Take this and hit it hard. Do as I say. We haven't much time. We must do it before the . . . the grease dries."

"But I thought you just wanted to play a joke on him," Barry protested. "Just so he wouldn't enter the race. I don't know if I really want to hurt his bike."

Barry stared at the liquid dripping near his feet. Grinsby shoved the hammer at him. Barry took it, his arms sagging under the weight.

"I don't care about the silly race, just hurry up," Grinsby commanded. "We haven't much time. Have another candy." Grinsby pulled a handful of Sweet Temptations from his pocket. He unwrapped two and stuffed them into Barry's greedy mouth. "Eat two. The flavor increases. Go on, we haven't much time."

Barry's doubts about hitting the Spirit Flyer suddenly melted away as the candies dissolved in his mouth. The flavor did increase.

"Now raise the hammer," Grinsby said. Barry did as he was instructed. "Now hit the front wheel. Smash it good."

"Shouldn't I get off first?" Barry asked, raising a leg to hop off the bike.

"No!" Grinsby shouted. "Do it now, you idiot. Hit the bike!"

Barry raised the hammer high above his head and began to swing it down. At that moment, the old bicycle suddenly jerked backward, throwing Barry off balance. He dropped the heavy hammer to the ground.

"What happened?" Barry asked. "Who pulled the bike?"

"No! I won't allow it," Grinsby screamed. He ran to pick up the hammer.

"What's going on?" Barry asked. He looked behind him to see who pulled the bike. All he saw was the dark street. Grinsby tried to give him the hammer, but when Barry reached for it, the Spirit Flyer jumped forward so suddenly that it almost knocked Barry off. This time the old red bicycle didn't stop but whizzed by Grinsby so close that he dove for cover under his truck. Then it continued down the dark street with Barry hanging on, screaming like a cat with its tail caught in a fan.

The Spirit Flyer shot up and down the deserted street so fast that all he could do was hold on. On his first scream, Barry swallowed the two candies. But they didn't go all the way down. They stuck in his throat. Barry tried to scream, but only made a gargling noise.

The old red bicycle shot around the corner like a rocket out of control. When Barry looked down, he saw that the wheels were four inches off the ground; he was flying! Barry's face went pale. He pushed back on the brake, but the old bike just went faster, turning the corner onto Elm Street.

Barry thought about jumping, but the ground was a blur below him; he was going too fast. Then he saw the large hole with the blinking yellow sign, "WARNING: KEEP AWAY." Barry stomped hard on the brake again, but the bike went faster. Barry's eyes opened wide with fear as he rushed toward the hole. Oh, why didn't I just stay in bed, Barry said to himself. He closed his eyes and waited for the crash, trying to scream. But the crash didn't happen. The Spirit Flyer shot straight for the hole, then at the last instant stopped dead in the air, four inches off the ground. Barry, however, kept going, flying off the seat, over the handlebars, over the blinking yellow sign and into the muddy brown pool of water. His final, wide-open scream died as his head plunged into the water. A few seconds later he surfaced, coughing and spitting out dirty water, which tasted and smelled like sewage. He grabbed the edge of the hole to pull himself out. But he slipped twice, falling back into the water. On the third try he crawled out. As he lay panting on the road, the warning sign blinked off and on, "WARNING: KEEP AWAY."

Then Barry noticed that the Spirit Flyer was gone. He stood up, his knees shaking, a dirty pool of water at his feet. He looked up and down the street. The old red bike was nowhere in sight. Barry shivered and sneezed; the smelly water ran in small rivers from his hair onto his face. The president of the Cobra Club resembled a sick, wet sewer rat. Barry sneezed again. On a bench by the side of the street a large black cat with green eyes stared at him.

"Get! Scat!" Barry said angrily. For some reason the cat bothered him. The cat continued staring, then opened its mouth wide, to show glistening sharp teeth. It hopped off the bench and ran straight toward Barry, mouth open.

Seeing the serious expression on the cat's face, Barry didn't wait around, but took off running down the street. He never looked back; he didn't slow down, even when his soggy sneaker slipped off his foot. Barry ran one-shoed the rest of the way home, leaving a trail of smelly water behind him.

THE DAY OF
THE BICYCLE
CONTESTS
· · · · · · · · ·

11

John Kramar woke up happy. Not only be-
cause it was the first day of summer vacation and the day of the bicycle
race, but more because he knew the Spirit Flyer was flying again. John
didn't care if he couldn't enter the Safety Contest; he could enter the
race. But even that didn't seem important. All he wanted was to have
the old red bicycle as his friend.

Susan, Katherine and Lois were excited too. All they could talk about
at breakfast was the bicycle contests and the race. Susan was going to
enter the Best-Looking Contest and race. Lois and Katherine were just
going to enter their small bikes in the Best-Looking Contest.

"My bike will come in first place," Katherine said. "Then Lois's bike in second place, then Susan's in third. It'll be wonderful."

"My bike will come in first," Lois said, "because I have a secret."

"We all might lose," Susan said. "But at least we can try."

"You aren't going to enter that old ugly bicycle of yours in the contest, are you, John?" Katherine asked. "If they had a contest for ugly bikes, it might win."

Lois and Katherine laughed hard. Even Susan smiled.

"Ha, ha," John said. " just wait and see."

Horace Grinsby didn't wake up that morning because he had not slept all night. When he saw the Spirit Flyer take off on its own power, he knew he would have to change his plans once again. He spent the rest of the night getting ready. While the Kramars were talking about the race, Grinsby was talking on the glowing red phone and sipping coffee.

"Yes, I realize that, sir," Grinsby was saying very politely. "But please try to realize the problems I'm having. We will try the Ransom Plan, then if that doesn't work . . . I hope we don't have to use the X-Removal Plan either. But as I have stated before, at least we are lucky that he hasn't put on the instruments. It's still in its primitive form. Plus if we can keep the boy separated, we have at least gained one . . ."

Grinsby listened to the voice shouting on the other end of the phone. He looked frightened for a moment.

"But sir, we succeeded so well until the truck incident," Grinsby stated. "I think I should receive some sort of recommendation for . . ."

Grinsby's face turned red as the phone screeched at him. He held it away from his ear, the noise was so loud.

"Yessir, I'm sorry, sir," Grinsby said, though he made a sour face at the phone. "I will keep you informed. I think the men I hired for today's job will be perfect. Both of them have just come out of one of their prisons. They have already been told what to do. Of course they are rather dull witted, but we can use that too."

Grinsby listened for a few minutes, then hung up. He climbed out of the truck. Two men dressed in gray janitor uniforms were leaning against the truck. One man was tall and skinny, the other short and chubby. They were drinking coffee and sucking on Sweet Temptations.

"Everything set?" Grinsby asked. "Is the truck ready?"

Both men nodded. The short man picked up a brown paper bag at his feet. He reached inside and pulled out a small pistol. The way he smiled made Grinsby feel uneasy.

"Put that away," Grinsby commanded. "You want the whole town to see you? I said you wouldn't need those."

"You take care of your business; I'll take care of mine," the short man grunted.

"Yeah," chimed in the tall, skinny man. "We ain't kids."

"Just be at the cafeteria at nine o'clock with the truck," Grinsby said. "Don't be late."

"We'll be there," the short man replied.

"Have some more candy," Grinsby said. He gave them several Sweet Temptations. "Eat two, the flavor increases."

The men put the candies in their mouths. They smiled, then began to laugh. Grinsby laughed too.

John dashed back to his room for his sneakers. In all the excitement, he'd put on his good shoes. Aunt Betty had left with his cousins for the school. Uncle Bill had left before breakfast.

John tied both his sneakers, then ran out to the garage. The moment he opened the door he sensed something was wrong. Then he saw it, or rather didn't see it. The Spirit Flyer was gone. John looked quickly around the garage. Maybe his uncle had moved it. John ran outside. But the bike wasn't there either. John began to feel scared. Where could the bike be? Maybe his uncle had taken it down to school for him. But John was sure Uncle Bill knew he wanted to ride the bike to school. Then the thought that John had been trying to avoid jumped into his mind; maybe the Spirit Flyer had been stolen! John felt the fear and panic rise in his chest, up to his throat.

He locked the garage door, then started running toward school.

Even though school was out, the school parking lot was filled with cars. It looked as if half the town was there. All the bikes for the Best-Looking Contest were inside the cafeteria. Almost every bicycle in town was entered.

John was breathing hard as he ran into the parking lot. He was late. A large tractor-trailer truck was backing up to the cafeteria kitchen door. John watched two men in gray uniforms get out of the truck. One man was tall and skinny, the other short and chubby. They walked to the back of the truck and went in the kitchen door. A long orange arrow was on the side of the truck.

John ran to the front of the school. He knew they were going to show a movie on bicycle safety in the auditorium. John ran down the empty halls. He stopped to walk, remembering it was against school rules to run in the halls. But then he ran again, feeling as if he had to talk to his uncle as soon as possible.

Just as John ran into the auditorium, the lights went out. A streak of light shot through the darkness; the movie on bicycle safety began. John searched through the rows of people trying to find his uncle. On the screen, a policeman was talking about hand signals. Then John saw Susan.

He scooted down the aisle, wriggled past people's legs and sat down in the seat next to his cousin.

"You finally got here!" Susan whispered excitedly. "Wait till you hear the news."

"Someone stole the Spirit Flyer," John said hurriedly. He didn't think Susan's news could be more important than that.

"I know," Susan said, lowering her voice.

"What? How can you know?" John asked. "I just found out before I came here."

"I heard Dad talking to Mr. Smedlowe," Susan replied. "Mr. Smedlowe found it in his garage this morning. Barry's tennis shoe was sitting on the seat. When Mr. Smedlowe showed Barry, Barry began screaming and saying strange things. Apparently Barry took it last night. Barry was so upset, Mr. Smedlowe said, that he didn't come to school today to race. Dad is going out there later to talk to him. I bet he's in real trouble this time."

John sat silently in the dark. He had suspected Horace Grinsby of being the thief, but he wasn't surprised that it was really Barry.

"Where's Grinsby?" John asked.

"He left just before the movie started," Susan whispered. "He was on the stage welcoming everyone, then he left to judge the bikes for the Best-Looking Contest."

"Where's the Spirit Flyer now?" John asked. "Did Mr. Smedlowe bring it to school?"

"I don't know," Susan said. "I didn't hear them say."

John settled back to watch the movie, but all he could think of was the Spirit Flyer. At least it's safe now, he thought.

As soon as the movie began, Horace Grinsby walked quickly to the cafeteria and locked the door. The tall man and the short man stood by the other door keeping guard.

"Ok, get to work," Grinsby said. "The film only lasts thirty minutes. I think we can get them all."

The two men put on gloves. The tall man grabbed two shiny ten-speed bicycles. With some difficulty he rolled them toward the door to the outside. The short man opened the door. The tall man pushed the bikes through the door, then up a ramp into the huge tractor-trailer truck. Grinsby was close behind with two more bicycles, a ten-speed and a five-speed dirt bike. The short man propped the door open, then began rolling bicycles into the truck too. They worked quietly but quickly. Grinsby occasionally checked his watch.

"This has to be one of the best heists I've ever made," the short man grunted. "These things are worth a fortune. And they're nice. A lot of them are new. How many do you suppose there are? A couple hundred?"

The tall man shrugged his shoulders and loaded two blue bikes into the truck. He piled bikes on top of each other to make more room. He had stopped counting how many he had loaded.

Grinsby smiled as he loaded two Goliath Cobras into the truck. He stopped, adjusted his derby, then looked at his watch; they would have time to get every bicycle.

"This will be like Christmas in reverse," the short man said. "I wish I could be around to see the brats' faces when they see this empty cafeteria."

"Just be quick," Grinsby reminded them. "We only have ten minutes left."

All three men continued working until the last bicycle was in the truck. A single handgrip with red streamers rested on the floor. Grinsby ran outside then returned with a long rope.

"Make it look good," Grinsby said. "But don't hurt me."

The short man tied Grinsby's legs, then his hands. Then he wrapped a blindfold around his eyes.

"Use the handkerchief in my pocket for a gag," Grinsby said. "Then get going. You know where to wait. And stay there. Don't get any foolish ideas."

"Sure, sure," the short man grunted. He jammed the handkerchief into Grinsby's mouth. A half minute later, the truck left. Grinsby laid back against the wall quietly, waiting to be discovered. The plan had worked so far.

The movie ended and Mr. Smedlowe talked a few minutes. Grinsby was supposed to wheel out the winning bicycle on the stage at the end of the movie. Then the Safety Contest would begin, followed by the race.

When Grinsby didn't show in five minutes, Sheriff Kramar went to investigate. A few minutes later he returned, his face filled with trouble. He walked straight to the microphone. Principal Smedlowe stood aside.

"I have an announcement," Sheriff Kramar said. "I don't know how to say this, but it appears as if all the bicycles entered in the Best-Looking Bicycle Contest have been stolen. Three men, according to Mr. Grinsby, tied him up and loaded the bicycles into a truck. That's all we know at this point."

Even Mr. Smedlowe's mouth dropped open. The crowd began to murmur, then talk louder. A small boy began to cry. Then someone else cried. The noise became a roar. Everybody talked at once.

"My bicycle!" Susan said. Her eyes filled with tears.

"Where did they put the Spirit Flyer?" John asked urgently. "I told you I don't know," Susan said. "But my bike was in the contest."

Lois, who was sitting on the other side of Susan, began to cry. She had put flowers in the basket of her little blue bicycle. Now it was gone. Other children cried. The grownups talked louder and louder.

"I've got to find the Spirit Flyer," John said. He pushed his way down the aisle. A crowd of people surrounded Sheriff Kramar. John couldn't even get close. The noise was so loud that nobody could hear. Finally, Mr. Kramar got the microphone and called for order. The crowd quieted.

"As of now, the Safety Contest and race are canceled," Sheriff Kramar announced. "I want everybody to write down your name and address, then a short description of your bicycle and its approximate value. One of our deputies will be at the door to collect this important information. Parents, please help your children. Pencils and paper are being brought to the auditorium right now. Please be patient."

John saw that it was impossible to talk to his uncle right away. He waited with Aunt Betty and his cousins in the lobby. One by one, grownups and children filed out of the auditorium, giving small slips of paper to the deputies. Most of the younger children had red eyes from crying. Roger walked through the doors looking sad.

"I guess they got mine too," he said. "I just got it for my birthday. I can't believe it. Practically the whole town got robbed. What about your bike?"

"I don't know," John said. "I have to talk to Uncle Bill." After another half hour, the long parade of sad faces thinned out. Sheriff Kramar, Mr. Smedlowe and Horace Grinsby walked out together.

". . . and I can't tell you how shocked and sorry I am," Grinsby was saying as the men walked into the lobby. "A great shock. A disgrace for the town and especially for your police department, Sheriff. I should have received better protection. I don't see how my company can be held responsible for this . . . this disgrace."

"Uncle Bill," John yelled, running over. "Where's my bicycle?"

Sheriff Kramar looked at Mr. Smedlowe. Mr. Smedlowe frowned.

"I forgot," Mr. Smedlowe said. "I have it locked in the trunk of my car."

"I'll still need to talk to Barry," Sheriff Kramar said. Neither man noticed the frown that crossed Horace Grinsby's face.

"If you gentlemen will excuse me," Grinsby said. "I need to make a report to my boss. He will be upset. Very upset. I guess all of us assumed that this county had a better sheriff's office."

"Maybe you should have been more cautious, Sheriff," Mr. Smedlowe said as they watched Grinsby stomp off. "That is your job after all. Your poor performance makes the school look bad. We'll be the laughing stock of the whole county. I hardly think Barry's minor involvement with your son's bicycle warrants attention. I'm sure it was some accident. He said he didn't bring the bicycle home. You need to remember who your friends are. I'm on the county board. There's sure to be an investigation into this whole incident."

"I'll still need to talk to Barry," Sheriff Kramar said coolly. "But it can wait until this afternoon. Just return John's bike, please."

John could tell that his uncle was angry. Mr. Smedlowe stormed out of the lobby. John ran after him. The principal glared at John as he opened the trunk of his car. The Spirit Flyer was lying on top of the spare tire.

Even though the old red bike was heavy, Mr. Smedlowe refused to help John lift it out.

"I haven't got all day, boy," Mr. Smedlowe said. "Let's go. And be careful not to scratch that fender."

With a mighty pull, John got the old bike out. Mr. Smedlowe grunted something, then slammed the trunk. John checked the bike carefully to see if it was damaged. If Barry had it, John knew anything was possible. But the old red bike seemed to be ok. John hopped on and rode it in a circle. Across the parking lot, his uncle waved at him. John rode over to see what he wanted.

"Ride the Spirit Flyer home right now and stay there, do you hear me?" Uncle Bill's face was lined with worry.

"But I wanted to . . ."

"No questions, John," Uncle Bill said. John could see by the look on his uncle's face that he shouldn't argue. "Get going. I'll be home in a few minutes. Go. Right now."

John turned and began pedaling home. What a day, he thought. What else could go wrong? John pedaled slowly. The day was too sunny and nice to be locked up in the house.

John wasn't home five minutes before the sheriff's car screeched to a halt outside the house. Aunt Betty waited by the door. She looked worried. John tried to question her, but she told him to wait for Uncle Bill.

"What's wrong?" John asked as Uncle Bill closed the door.

"Read this," Uncle Bill said. He gave John a slip of white paper. The words were written in red ink.

To John Kramar:

Give up the Spirit Flyer! Cut it in three pieces and put it outside the sheriff's office by noon tomorrow. All the bikes taken today will be returned. Don't be foolish. Destroy the Spirit Flyer.

REMEMBER
JOE
. . . .
12

"What does it mean?" John asked. "Why would they want me to destroy the Spirit Flyer?"

"I'm not sure," Uncle Bill said, shaking his head in frustration. "I'm just not sure."

The telephone rang. Aunt Betty picked it up.

"Hello?" she said. She listened. "Yes, there was a note. And that was the demand . . . What are we going to do? . . . I'm not sure, Mrs. Hillsby . . . Yes, I know the other bikes are very valuable, . . . and your son's bike was stolen too? I'm sorry to hear that. We'll let you know what we decide . . . Really, Mrs. Hillsby, I don't think that's being fair to Bill. Yes, but . . ."

Aunt Betty put the telephone down. She looked uneasily at Uncle Bill.

"News travels fast, it seems," she said. "That was Mrs. Hillsby. She heard about the note from Mrs. Smedlowe. She thinks John should destroy the Spirit Flyer right now. She also made a rather nasty remark about Centerville's sheriff's office doing a bad job. She even offered to help destroy the Spirit Flyer herself. She says she knows how to use a welding torch. Can you imagine? Then she hung up."

Uncle Bill started to say something, but the phone rang again.

"I'll get this one," he said. "Hello? . . . Yes, Mr. Barrows, we are all upset . . . Yes, there was a note. And it did mention my nephew's bicycle . . . The sheriff's office is considering an appropriate response . . . I personally don't think we should bargain with thieves . . . I realize the stolen bicycles are worth a lot of money . . . No, I'm not sure what my nephew's bicycle is worth. It might be an antique . . . Yes . . . I understand." He hung up.

"Well, that was Mr. Barrows," Uncle Bill said. "He wants to take up a collection from the town and pay John to destroy the Spirit Flyer. He said Mr. Grinsby suggested the idea."

"But they can't!" John protested. "I don't want their money. I want the Spirit Flyer. It's magic. It flies. It saved my life yesterday. It flew over a pickup truck. You can ask Roger. Or Barry Smedlowe. He tried to make me run into a hole on Elm Street."

"We're not going to go through a flying-bicycle discussion again," Uncle Bill said firmly. "I have enough problems already. I want you all to go into the kitchen and make cookies or something. You are not to leave the house, John. I want you to put the Spirit Flyer in your bedroom and leave it there. "Whoever's trying to get it might be dangerous."

"But Uncle Bill," John said, "it really did . . ."

The phone rang. Uncle Bill answered. "Hello? . . . Yes . . . Yes . . . There was a note; that's correct . . . That's what it said, more or less. Hold on for a moment, please." Uncle Bill covered the mouthpiece with his hand. "Please go to the kitchen. Everybody."

"Ok, let's go," Aunt Betty said. "It's time to make cookies."

"Can't I stay?" John asked, looking at his uncle. Uncle Bill shook his head. John left the room dragging his feet. "Who wants to make dumb old cookies at a time like this?"

Horace Grinsby was talking on the phone too. He had a big smile on his face. He smoked a big cigar, carefully tapping the ashes into his coffee cup.

"It went as smooth as a snake's belly," Grinsby said, then chuckled. "I left soon after I was assured the note had been received. I casually suggested setting up a fund. The idea was a success, of course. I plan to go by the sheriff's office a little later. First, I need to see the Smedlowe boy. He might be a problem, but I'll take care of him. By this time tomorrow I should be able to deliver the Spirit Flyer, at least what's left of it." Grinsby laughed out loud. "With the other bikes gone, we'll be able to start the Toy Campaign. These poor idiots will never feel a thing."

Grinsby laughed some more and listened some more. Finally he hung up the glowing phone. He tapped more ashes into his coffee cup, then poured in a hot liquid from a black bottle. Smoke bubbled up out of the cup. Grinsby smiled and drank the whole mixture in one gulp. He burped, then started the truck.

In two minutes he was in front of the Smedlowes' house. Barry was outside watering a rosebush with a green hose. Grinsby walked quickly across the lawn.

"Well, young man, I hear you're in trouble," Grinsby said, grinning broadly. Barry tried to smile but couldn't. He was afraid of the strange man in the black derby, especially when he remembered the way Grinsby looked the night before, holding the hammer. Grinsby took a Sweet Temptation out of his pocket, peeled the wrapper and popped the candy into his mouth. He sucked on it slowly. Barry's mouth began to water.

"You are in trouble too," Barry accused. "You made me steal it. It was your idea."

"I made you what?" Grinsby asked. "Don't be ridiculous. Who would believe a silly story like that?"

"Sheriff Kramar," Barry said defiantly.

"And what would you tell him?"

"That you paid me to steal the bike."

"Have I paid you anything?" Grinsby asked.

"No," Barry said. "But you were going to if I stole the bike and gave it to you. But I couldn't because . . ."

"Because why?" Grinsby asked. He smiled, then took another candy out of his pocket. Barry looked hungrily at the candy.

"Because it took off down the street and almost killed me," Barry said. "It wasn't even on the ground. That crazy bike flew. It *flew!* Then it dumped me in that big wet hole on Elm Street. I almost drowned."

"Really?" Grinsby asked. "Then what happened?"

"I don't know," Barry said. "It disappeared. But my dad found it in our garage this morning."

"And who is going to believe a story like that?" Grinsby asked, chuckling to himself. "A flying bicycle? A disappearing bicycle? A bicycle that moves by itself? Really?"

"But you saw it move last night," Barry protested.

"I didn't see anything last night except television, young man," Grinsby said. "I was in my motel room all evening watching television. Here. Have a candy."

Barry took the Sweet Temptation even though he absolutely hated Grinsby at that moment. He suddenly realized how strange his story would sound. Barry stuck the candy into his mouth. Somehow the sweet tasted even sweeter than he remembered. He felt better. Without witnesses, it was his word against Grinsby's. Barry doubted if anyone would believe his story. Grinsby would deny everything. Barry almost didn't care, the candy tasted so good.

"Can I have another piece?" Barry asked.

"Certainly," Grinsby said. He smiled broadly. "But first we need to make sure what story we are going to tell. I suggest you say you were playing a little game on the Kramar boy and that you intended to give the bicycle back the next day, no harm done. Isn't that how it *really* happened?"

"Well, sort of, I guess," Barry said uneasily. He knew he didn't have a chance of convincing anyone of the truth. He wasn't sure what had happened anyway. He had been tired and it was late and dark. And the more he sucked on the strange green and red candy, the less he cared what had really happened. "If I say all of that, can I have more candy?"

"Certainly, lad, certainly," Grinsby said. "What are friends for?"

Making sure no one was watching, Grinsby took a white envelope out of his pocket. He gave it to Barry.

"This is just a little token of friendship, boy," Grinsby said. "Just to help you remember what *really* happened. With all the problems of today, the sheriff probably won't even worry about your little practical joke."

Barry looked inside the envelope.

"Wow!" Barry said, trying to count the money. "How much is there?"

"Just enough so we're good, good friends," Grinsby said, slapping Barry on the back. "And of course, that's never quite enough, so once we're sure the sheriff knows about your little practical joke and that you didn't mean any harm, there'll be a few more envelopes, just like that one."

"What about the candy? Can I have more candy too?" Barry asked greedily.

"Of course, lad. What are friends for?" Grinsby pulled a whole sack out of his suit pocket. "Don't eat too much at once. It can be dangerously delicious."

"Who cares?" Barry said, stuffing two pieces into his mouth. "I could eat this stuff all day."

"So you shall, lad," Grinsby said, chuckling. "Some day you shall."

Barry didn't even notice Grinsby speed away. He was too busy counting his money and the pieces of candy. Grinsby smiled inside his truck
as he picked up the glowing red phone to make his report.

No one had much of an appetite that night at supper in the Kramar
house. Even though Aunt Betty had made fried chicken, John's favorite
dish, John didn't even eat a whole drumstick. After all the plates were
cleared away, Uncle Bill stood up.

"Well, it's been a horrible day," he sighed. "The thieves seem to have
gotten away without a clue. An all-points bulletin is out, but it doesn't
look good. If we had more time . . ."

"Does that mean John will have to destroy the Spirit Flyer like the
ransom note said?" Susan asked. Everyone looked at Uncle Bill.

"That's the most disturbing part about this whole business," Uncle
Bill said. "It doesn't make sense. If they didn't demand that you *destroy*
the Spirit Flyer, maybe I would understand. What good is that old bike
if it's destroyed? Now if they offered to *trade* the stolen bicycles for the
Spirit Flyer, then I would assume it's worth more than we know. Horace
Grinsby offered a thousand dollars. He would even be a suspect in this
case if the thieves wanted to trade, but they don't."

"I don't like him," John said. "He's always smiling, and he acts nice,
but I don't think he's nice. I think he's creepy."

"So far Mr. Grinsby has been very helpful, in a way," Uncle Bill said.
"In fact, he's offered to chip in five hundred dollars on the ransom
fund."

"The what?" Susan asked.

"The ransom fund," Uncle Bill said. "Mr. Grinsby even sort of started
it. Once word got around about the note, Mr. Grinsby offered five
hundred dollars to pay John to destroy the Spirit Flyer. He thought that
was only fair, he said. Almost everyone in town contributed a little
money. The last time I heard it was close to nine hundred dollars."

"You mean they're going to make me destroy the Spirit Flyer?" John asked. He couldn't believe his ears. "I don't want their old money. Tell them I won't do it. Tell them, Uncle Bill. I'll never destroy the Spirit Flyer. Even if they gave me a million dollars."

Uncle Bill looked sadly at his wife. She looked down at the table.

"I certainly don't intend to bargain with bicycle thieves," Uncle Bill said. "On the other hand, I'm responsible to the people of this county. They look to me to protect them and their property. Today they became as bad as a lynch mob. The value of those bicycles is over twenty-five thousand dollars, not counting sentimental value. Those bicycles were Christmas presents and birthday gifts, nickels and dimes saved in piggy banks. Everyone wants their bicycle. And they think the Spirit Flyer is a cheap price to pay. To them, nine hundred dollars for a beat-up old bicycle is very reasonable. I tried to tell them that even if John destroyed the Spirit Flyer, the thieves might not return the other bicycles. Why should they do what they say? They're thieves. But you can't reason with a mob. The office was a madhouse today, people shouting and screaming. Mr. Grinsby was taking donations for the ransom fund outside on the steps and giving everyone candy like we were having a party. I suppose he was just trying to help."

"I had to take the phone off the hook, so many people kept calling," Aunt Betty said. "Everyone knew about the note. And some of our nicest friends were downright rude. Evil just brings out more evil in people."

"I don't want to destroy the Spirit Flyer," John said. He felt a lump in his throat. He knew he was ready to cry. Uncle Bill shook his head.

"This whole thing has got me confused," he said. "There's no law that says John has to give up his bike. Yet we have to live with these people. The town is crying out for blood. I've never seen anything like it. And it's all over *bicycles,* especially that old, beat-up Spirit Flyer. I just don't . . ."

"Look!" screeched Lois. "The telephone is blinking!"

"What?" Uncle Bill asked.

Everyone turned around. The red telephone near the refrigerator was glowing off and on like the blinking taillight of a car. The receiver was off the hook so it couldn't ring. Yet the whole telephone, even the curly wire, throbbed on and off, blink, blink, as if it had a life of its own.

"Why, that's the craziest thing I've . . ." Uncle Bill's voice trailed off. The whole family stood around the eerily glowing phone. Blink, blink, blink.

"Is it talking?" Lois asked.

"Of course not," Uncle Bill said. "It's impossible with the receiver off the hook. Maybe there's an electrical overload on the line. I'm sure there's a reasonable, logical explanation."

"Maybe it's haunted," Katherine said. "Mommie, I'm scared."

"There's nothing to be scared of," Uncle Bill said. He grabbed the receiver and held it up. The red throbbing glow continued in his hand. "See, there's nothing to be . . ."

But at that instant, a strange creaking noise came out of the phone, like the sound of an old door opening.

"Mommiiiie!" Katherine whined. Aunt Betty put her hand around Katherine's shoulder. But everyone kept staring at the glowing telephone.

Then they heard the sound of someone sighing. Suddenly a voice whispered, as if it came from a faraway, ancient grave, "Destroy the Spirit Flyer . . . Remember Joe."

The phone stopped glowing. Uncle Bill dropped the phone as if it burned. Katherine screamed.

WORK
TO DO
• • • • • • • •
13

All the girls demanded that they sleep in their parents' bedroom that night. Right after the voice on the telephone, Uncle Bill ordered everyone to bed. Each girl took her sleeping bag and camped on the floor. John wanted to get his sleeping bag too, but there wasn't enough room. While Uncle Bill called the telephone company, Aunt Betty tucked in the children.

"Something bad is happening, isn't it?" Susan said softly so only her mother would hear.

"Don't scare your sisters," Aunt Betty said. "I'm not sure what's going on, but it doesn't look good."

John felt very much alone in his room. He had too many questions rushing through his mind to get any sleep. The voice on the phone made him feel cold. He put on a sweater even though it was a warm June evening. Then he got in bed and read one of his favorite books. His uncle had left the house suddenly after talking on the phone. John was determined to stay awake and question him when he got home. But at nine-thirty Aunt Betty made him turn out the light. John lay in the darkness, the old red bicycle at the foot of his bed, and waited.

Much, much later, he heard a door slam. He wasn't sure if he had fallen asleep or not. Quietly, he crept down the hall to the living room. His aunt and uncle were talking on the sofa in whispers. John tried to hear.

". . . and they acted like *I* was crazy," Uncle Bill said. "They said the lines might have gotten crossed, but nothing could make the phone glow."

"But it said, 'Remember Joe,' " Aunt Betty whispered. "That call was to us. How could anyone, . . . *why* would anyone say such a thing?"

"I don't know," Uncle Bill said. He sounded very tired. "I went out to his old workshop and looked around in his things. I couldn't find any clues."

John couldn't hear well enough, so he leaned closer, poking his head underneath a small table by the door. But as he moved, he knocked the table leg, which made the lamp on top shake.

"Come out, John," Uncle Bill said.

John scooted out from the table and stood up, feeling foolish, yet defiant. He wasn't sure if he was in trouble or not.

"I couldn't sleep and I wanted to know what happened," John said quickly. "Why did the telephone act like that?"

"We don't know," Uncle Bill said. "But you shouldn't be eavesdropping on our conversation."

"But I want to know what's going on," John complained. "Nobody tells me anything, and it's my bicycle. The voice on the phone said something about Joe. Did it mean my father?"

Mr. and Mrs. Kramar looked at each other. They both seemed upset, maybe even afraid. Uncle Bill shook his head back and forth slowly.

"I just don't know," he said. "Maybe. But if the voice was referring to your father, you could be in great danger."

"Why?" John asked. "What have I done?"

"I don't think it's what you've done but more who you are," Uncle Bill said. "And what you have, namely, the Spirit Flyer."

"I don't understand," John said.

"Well, none of us understand," Uncle Bill said. He sighed. "Maybe there's no connection to your father. I wish my dad was here. He might have some ideas."

"Does Grandfather Kramar know something?" John asked.

"He might," Uncle Bill said. "Anyway, we can't call him until tomorrow. Let's all just go to bed. In the morning we can call. We'll still have time to think things over before noon."

"Will I have to destroy the Spirit Flyer?" John asked.

"I hope not," Uncle Bill said. "Now let's all just get some sleep and pray for the best."

John didn't think he'd ever fall asleep; he kept asking himself the same questions again and again. Why did someone want him to destroy the Spirit Flyer? Was the old bike really valuable? Was he really in danger? What kind of danger? And did the voice on the phone mean Joe, his father? John stared at the ceiling, thinking and thinking until he fell into an uneasy sleep.

John dreamed several things. Once again he was riding the Spirit Flyer high above the clouds toward the open mouth of the giant black snake. Someone was calling his name. John tried to scream back an answer, saying, "I'm here; I'm here." But he couldn't. No sound came out of his mouth. He felt as if he was suffocating. Then suddenly the dream changed and John felt he was all right, that someone was helping him. John was riding the Spirit Flyer through beautiful blue skies. Below him was a farm. A man in a field waved a hat at him in friendly welcome. Then John recognized the man—Grandfather Kramar! John shouted and steered the Spirit Flyer down to him. John felt happy and full of peace. His grandfather was smiling. As the old red bike glided down next to his grandfather, John started to hop off. But his grandfather said, "Wait. Wake up. There's work to do."

Then John was back in his bed. Someone was shaking him awake. John opened his eyes, mumbling. He looked around the room to see who had shaken him. The Spirit Flyer rested on its kickstand near the bed.

"Who shook me?" John asked, thinking maybe one of his cousins was playing a joke. He looked on the floor, but no one was hiding. He started to look under the bed when the Spirit Flyer rolled forward and gently bumped his leg. John blinked twice. Suddenly he was very awake.

"So it was you," John said.

Then all by itself, the bike turned around and rolled toward the closed door of his bedroom. John watched in amazement as the old bike's front tire bumped against the door, then backed away. At that instant the door opened by itself. The Spirit Flyer rolled out into the hall.

The old red bike paused for a moment, as if waiting for him, then rolled down the hall without a sound. The boy quickly put on his slippers then ran after the old bike.

"Where are you going?" John whispered, following the Spirit Flyer through the house to the back door of the kitchen. The old bike bumped the back door. The door opened. The Spirit Flyer rolled outside to the lawn, stopping on the grass.

John walked outside, shutting the back door quietly. He stared at the old red bike, unsure what to do.

"Do you want to go somewhere?" John asked. He walked over to the bike. He felt chilly, standing in the damp grass, dressed only in his pajamas and slippers. Nevertheless, he climbed onto the seat of the old bicycle.

He wondered if he should start pedaling, but the old bicycle began moving by itself across the lawn. John held onto the handlebars. He didn't try to steer it; the old red bicycle seemed to know where it wanted to go. After rolling a few feet, it left the ground, rising swiftly into the air, gaining speed as it passed over nearby houses. The wheels were turning, but John wasn't pedaling. Even though he was chilly, John felt wonderful, speeding quietly through the air, the lights of Centerville blinking below him. To the east, the sky was lighter; dawn was coming to push away the night.

The old red bike kept going higher and higher. It flew over Centerville, out past the river into the farm country. At first John thought the old bike might be taking him to Grandfather Kramar's farm, like in his dream. But they were going in the opposite direction.

The boy and bicycle passed over several farms and forests. Then the Spirit Flyer began to descend. They skimmed over the tops of trees out in the middle of nowhere, it seemed to John. Then in a small clearing, John saw an old farmhouse and barn. As they flew silently closer, John could see by the old broken windows of the house that it had been abandoned a long time ago. The Spirit Flyer suddenly slowed down.

The old red bike moved above the barn, then slowly dropped down, landing on the roof. John immediately assumed the bike wasn't going to move, so he got off to explore. The old barn roof creaked under his feet; the shingles were rotten. Suddenly John's leg slipped and dropped through the roof. Luckily, he only scraped his leg. As he examined his wound, he noticed something in the barn. Through the hole in the roof, he saw a shiny tractor-trailer truck parked inside.

"Now why would a nice truck like that be parked in this old barn?" John asked aloud. Then his heart skipped a beat. An orange arrow was on the side of the truck. The bicycle thieves! John crawled quickly to the Spirit Flyer and climbed on.

He took a firm grip on the handlebars, pulled down, then started to pedal. But the pedals wouldn't turn!

"Come on!" John said. "Let's go."

He pushed harder on the pedals. Finally they moved slowly, as if they were turning in a bowl of glue.

"Please," John said, "we don't have much time. We need to go right now, before they get away."

But the old red bike had other plans in mind. It moved about six inches. John stopped fighting it; it was too hard.

"Good grief," John said disgustedly. "You bring me out here; then you don't help me. I guess I'll have to do this by myself. Maybe I can drive the truck back. But I don't know these roads. I could get lost. And I don't even know how to drive. What kind of mess have you gotten me into? You bring me out to the middle of nowhere and abandon me."

John was beginning to feel angry. Of course he wasn't really abandoned; he was sitting right on top of the Spirit Flyer. But John was young and didn't know the secrets of the old red bike. He liked to fly, but he didn't like to wait.

"If that's the way it is, I'll figure something out by myself," John said defiantly. He started to get off the old bike, but when he lifted his foot, it wouldn't leave the pedal. John shook his foot. It was stuck. He shook it harder. Nothing happened. Then he pulled and shook at the same time. But his foot remained on the pedal. Then John realized that by some magic the old red bicycle wouldn't let his foot loose.

Instead of trusting the Spirit Flyer, the boy became angrier. He jerked his foot as hard as he could, but once again, nothing happened.

"Let me go!" John commanded. "I can do this without your help."

Immediately John's foot came off the pedal. He grunted and knocked the kickstand down. He almost kicked the old bike because he was angry, but he remembered what had happened the last time he had kicked the Spirit Flyer. He didn't want the tires to go flat, at least not on top of the barn.

John got down on his hands and knees. Very carefully, he crawled along the roof, avoiding holes and rusty nails. The boards creaked and popped. John peered through a large hole trying to find a way down into the barn. Far below him he saw the floor. Maybe I should go back to the Spirit Flyer, John thought. Then he saw a rope attached to an old pulley on a rafter. In his eagerness to get to the rope, John crawled too quickiy onto some shingles that *seemed* solid. Suddenly there was a groan, then a terrific crack. The next thing he knew, he was falling through the air.

THE PARADE AT SIX IN THE MORNING

14

John screamed, twisting in the air. His mouth was open when he hit the ground. He felt a prickling sensation and plunged into darkness; the falling stopped. If I'm dead, he thought, it doesn't hurt very much, but it sure itches. Then he realized that he wasn't dead at all, but had fallen into a pile of hay. He sputtered, spitting the hay out of his mouth, then clawed for daylight.

John had just poked his head out when he heard voices. A small door opened. John burrowed quickly back into the hay, covering his head.

"I know I heard a scream," a man's voice said.

"You were just dreaming," a different voice answered. "Let's get some sleep. It's only five-thirty in the morning. It's bad for my health to be up this early."

A straw was poking into John's nose, but he was afraid to move. He could hear steps close to the hay pile. Then it was too late. He knew he was going to sneeze.

"Aaaachoo!"

"Bless you," a man's voice said. "Hey!"

Suddenly a hand grabbed John's shoulder and yanked him out of the hay pile. John recognized the tall man and short man instantly. He had seen them at the school cafeteria yesterday just before the robbery. The short man held a long pitchfork whose sharp prongs were two inches from John's stomach.

"Where'd you come from, kid?" the short man asked. He shoved the pitchfork closer. John didn't say anything; he was too scared.

"Why is he in pajamas?" the tall man asked. "This is a weird kid."

John looked down at himself. He'd forgotten all about his pajamas. He suddenly wished he was safe on the Spirit Flyer. He looked up. Through the hole where he had fallen, he saw the Spirit Flyer still parked on the roof. The tall man looked up too.

"Hey, there's a bicycle on the roof," the tall man said.

"You got bicycles on the brain," the short man said. "Why would there be a bicycle on the roof?"

"Look for yourself," the tall man said. "It's a red bicycle, and . . . hey, it's moving!"

The short man looked up. John saw it too. The Spirit Flyer was slowly rising straight into the air.

"It stopped," the short man said. "What's holding it up?"

Before the tall man could speak, the Spirit Flyer suddenly dove down, crashing through the rotten boards of the roof. Like a dive-bombing eagle, the old red bike aimed straight for the thieves. Both men screamed and fell to the ground as it swooped over their heads. The short man held up the pitchfork when he saw the Spirit Flyer turn around in the air. As the old bike dived again, the short man jabbed the pitchfork at the front tire. But the instant the pitchfork touched, sparks jumped and sizzled; the prongs of the pitchfork glowed red, then melted like wax.

The short man screamed, dropping the pitchfork. The Spirit Flyer flew high into the rafters, then dropped slowly through the air, landing on top of the truck. Everything was quiet. The two men stood up, never taking their eyes off the old bicycle.

Suddenly the silence was broken by the sound of the truck engine starting up. The men looked at each other in surprise, then ran to the truck.

"Turn it off!" the short man hollered as the tall man jumped into the driver's seat.

"How can I?" the tall man shouted. "The keys aren't in it."

"Let me see," the short man said, pushing the tall man aside. As both men struggled to sit in the seat, the driver's door began to close behind them.

"Stop pushing me!" the short man yelled.

"I'm not doing anything," the tall one answered. "The door's pushing me. This crazy truck is haunted!"

The two thieves tried to push the door open, but the magic was stronger. The door slammed shut, locking them inside.

At that moment, the Spirit Flyer rose into the air, then stopped. The truck engine roared. The men inside screamed. Suddenly the truck jumped forward, smashing through the tall wooden doors of the barn. Pieces of wood flew in all directions.

Once outside, the truck stopped, the engine humming. The Spirit Flyer dropped quietly to the ground. John ran over to the old red bicycle and climbed on. But nothing happened. He tried to pedal, but once again the pedals wouldn't move. John almost said something mean to the old bike when he realized that he should just wait.

"I'm sorry I didn't trust you," John said.

As if answering, the Spirit Flyer rose in the air. It flew forward and landed on top of the trailer, right behind the cab. John heard the two thieves arguing inside, pounding on the doors and windows.

The truck started to move. With John and the Spirit Flyer on top, the truck pulled out of the farmyard. It turned onto an old dirt road and sped up. The dirt road was full of holes, but the truck went fast. The men inside the cab screamed and yelled, but they couldn't stop the truck or steer it. The truck was moving by a power the thieves had never known.

John wasn't sure where the truck was going. But when they finally reached the paved highway, the truck turned by itself and headed toward Centerville. The truck moved so fast John wondered if it wasn't flying too. All he knew was that the Spirit Flyer had caught the bicycle thieves. And that meant he wouldn't have to destroy the old red bike.

The truck just went faster and faster. Far down the highway John saw the familiar water tower of Centerville. Within five minutes the speeding truck entered the town limits.

The truck slowed down once it drove into town. Since it was early in the morning, not many people were awake. But that soon changed. When the truck turned onto Main Street, the loud air horn began to blow, Whaaaaaaaaaaaaaaaaaaaaa.

The horn continued to blow and the truck drove up and down the neighborhood streets as if it were in a parade. But most people aren't happy to hear a loud, noisy parade at six o'clock on Saturday morning. As the truck moved slowly down the streets, the horn blaring, people stormed out of their houses to see what was making the noise. When they saw John sitting on the Spirit Flyer on top of the big truck, they stared in amazement. John didn't know what to do, and so he just smiled and waved. Some of the little children waved back, but most of the adults just frowned.

"I've got the stolen bicycles!" John yelled. When the children heard that, they ran after the slow-moving truck. Soon a large parade of children and grownups were following the truck like a ragged tail. As John

passed his own house, Aunt Betty ran outside wearing her bathrobe. Katherine, Lois and Susan came outside too. They joined the parade of people following the truck. The noise of the horn and the people got louder.

Soon John heard a siren. Uncle Bill was already on his morning patrol. The sheriff's car came down the street in the opposite direction, the red lights flashing. Uncle Bill got out of the car and stared in disbelief as the truck passed by. He shouted something, but John couldn't hear over the noise of the horn and the crowd.

Sheriff Kramar turned the car around and followed the truck. More and more people came out of their houses and joined the crowd. The truck turned down Maple Street, went a few more blocks, and stopped in front of the sheriff's office. The loud horn shut off. And when the horn stopped, all the people quieted down.

Sheriff Kramar got out of the car. He was the only person in the crowd not dressed in pajamas or a bathrobe.

"Uncle Bill!" John shouted. "The bicycles are in the truck. And the thieves are inside the cab."

Sheriff Kramar opened the driver's door of the truck, his gun drawn. But right away he could see that he wouldn't need it. The thieves were huddled on the floor of the truck, shaking and trembling, a wild look in their eyes.

"Take me, please, take me," the tall man begged. "I'm guilty. Just get me away from this spooky truck and that crazy bicycle."

The short man couldn't even speak. He mumbled something as he crawled out, his eyes staring off into space. He held up his hands.

"This is a weird town," the tall man said as he looked at the crowd of people dressed in their pajamas and bathrobes. "A really weird town."

One of the deputies, dressed in pajamas like everyone else, led the two frightened men into the jail.

Sheriff Kramar walked to the back of the truck. He opened the doors slowly. Inside was a mountain of shiny handlebars, black tires and colorful frames—the stolen bicycles!

When the townspeople saw the bicycles, a cheer went up. The noise became even louder than before. John sat on the Spirit Flyer and smiled. They were cheering for him.

THE
X-REMOVAL
PLAN
• • • • • • • •
15

Not everyone in Centerville was cheering. While the townspeople were applauding the return of the stolen bicycles, Horace Grinsby was sucking bitterly on a Sweet Temptation, waiting for the phone call he knew would come. The red phone began glowing almost immediately. Grinsby picked it up.

"Good morning, sir, I was just about to—"

The cold voice on the other end of the phone screamed at him in fury. Grinsby winced.

"Yessir, but . . . but . . ." Grinsby feebly protested. "I realize that, sir, but I had no idea that . . ."

Grinsby shut up. He listened to the voice. He became more and more angry.

"But sir, you know the cloud they have put around this idiot boy," Grinsby protested. "I say get rid of him. We lose in one sense, yet he can't do any more damage . . . if we allow him to continue, who knows . . ."

The dark voice screamed once more. Smoke began pouring from the earpiece of the telephone. Grinsby coughed.

"You've made your point, sir," Grinsby said, choking. "I will proceed with the X-Removal Plan. But I take no responsibility for it. If it fails, you'll have to speak to the Boss about it. I think I can prevent him from seeing the grandfather. But if that happens, then what will . . ."

Grinsby was covered by the smoke pouring from the glowing telephone. His red eyes watered; tears streamed down his face.

"I will proceed, sir," Grinsby said. "But I still say, let's kill the . . ."

But the phone stopped glowing before Grinsby finished. He slammed it down on the hook and stared out the window. Down the street, the boy was still on top of the truck. The sheriff was returning the bicycles to the happy owners.

"I'll fix you all," Grinsby swore, then coughed. He climbed into the back of his truck. He pulled a blanket off a large black box that looked like a safe, only it didn't appear to have a door. "I'll fix you good," he said.

He didn't chuckle.

John Kramar could hardly hear himself think, so many people were congratulating him. All the townspeople were crowded around the truck, calling to him, asking him questions.

"How did you do it?" someone asked.

"Did they put up a fight?"

"Were you afraid?"

"Did you use a gun?"

"He deserves a reward. He's a regular hero. Where's the photographer?"

And on and on. John tried to answer the questions at first, but nobody seemed to be listening. A photographer from the town newspaper took some pictures. John smiled, beginning to feel like a hero. But on the second picture, the Spirit Flyer rolled onto John's toe just as the photographer snapped the picture.

"Ooooch!" John said. He pushed the bike off his toe. John smiled once more for the camera, standing on the edge of the roof of the truck. But this time, just as the photographer pressed the button, the old red bike rolled forward again, knocking John's leg.

"WhoooooOaaaaa!" John screamed as he lost his balance and fell.

"Look out!" the crowd yelled. "Catch him!"

For the second time that day John was falling. Luckily, he didn't fall far. A dozen arms caught him and stood him on his feet.

"He's kind of a clumsy hero, I'd say," a voice in the crowd said. Everyone laughed. John's face turned red. He felt ridiculous. He almost felt angry. He knew the Spirit Flyer had pushed him on purpose.

Two men got the old red bike off the top of the truck. Once on the ground, John sat on the seat. The photographer wanted to take some more pictures. The crowd stood back.

"How's this for a headline, Jake?" someone yelled. "Boy Hero Saves Bicycles, Then Falls Off Truck!"

The crowd laughed. John turned red again. Then he suddenly noticed the black truck of Horace Grinsby parked down the street. The door opened and smoke poured out for a second. When the smoke stopped, Grinsby got out and looked at the crowd. Even though he was too far away to see clearly, John had an eerie feeling that Grinsby was looking right at him and the Spirit Flyer. All the happiness he felt about having brought back the stolen bicycles seemed to vanish. John suddenly felt uneasy and scared. Something was wrong, yet he wasn't sure what.

"I need to talk to Uncle Bill," John said to the crowd of townspeople.

"Just one more picture," the photographer said.

John suddenly shivered. For some reason he felt cold, even though the sun was shining. John waited for the photographer, trying to smile. Down the street, he saw Grinsby walking toward him. Maybe I need to be dressed in real clothes, John thought to himself, looking down at his pajamas. Maybe that's why I'm cold.

Sheriff Kramar was also surrounded by a crowd. Each person was more impatient than the next to get his or her bicycle back. Everyone talked at once. John felt sorry for his uncle. I never want to be sheriff, he thought to himself. People always complain; they're never happy with one thing or another, yet they want the sheriff to keep them safe all the time. John looked at all the talking faces. These same people who were calling him a hero now would have made him destroy the Spirit Flyer yesterday.

Grinsby walked closer to the crowd. As he got closer, John saw that Grinsby *was* staring right at him and the Spirit Flyer. The boy felt another cold wave of fear pass over him. Grinsby kept walking, slowly. John stared back at the dark man. His eyes look awful, John thought. They look so red, almost as if . . . John blinked twice and looked at Grinsby again. For a moment he thought Grinsby's eyes actually glowed red.

"Smile, John," the photographer said.

But John didn't hear. He stared at Grinsby's pale face. Then he saw it for sure; Grinsby's eyes glowed red, like two small lights.

"Hey, John, get ready and smile when I say cheese," the photographer said.

Suddenly the Spirit Flyer began to move. John was startled at first, but held on. His feet were on the pedals as they went around, so it looked like he was pedaling, only John knew that he wasn't.

"Where are you going?" the photographer shouted.

But the old red bike sped up, pulling away from the crowd. John glanced back at Grinsby. The man in the black derby stopped walking and looked at John. The Spirit Flyer kept moving on the ground. The noise of the crowd faded away as he turned the corner on Elm Street.

John took his feet off the pedals, but the old red bicycle whizzed along by itself. The bike turned the corner onto John's street and headed for his home. John thought the Spirit Flyer would stop once it got to his house, but it only went faster and faster, as if it were in a hurry. John began to feel cold again. Maybe I should go home and change clothes, he said to himself. John turned around to look back.

Horace Grinsby's black truck was only fifty feet behind him, going fast. John saw two red lights glowing behind the windshield. The truck sped up. John felt colder. For some reason he wanted to jump off and run. The truck came closer and closer. The red eyes glowed at John. The truck was so close John could see Grinsby's face. Only it wasn't his face; it was the face of someone dead—a pale shriveled mask of a face with its teeth bared, snarling like a rabid dog.

Suddenly the Spirit Flyer lifted up into the air. John was almost frozen with sweat. The speeding black truck shot underneath the boy and bicycle, just missing them. The brakes squealed in failure. The bike soared higher and faster into the air. Something evil was in Grinsby's truck. And Grinsby. He must have been wearing an old Halloween mask, John thought. In his mind he could still see the red glowing eyes, the bared teeth. John held on tighter as the red bicycle soared higher, leaving Centerville far behind.

Inside the black truck two hands carefully put on the plastic face of Horace Grinsby. The red eyes stopped glowing but appeared bloodshot and watery. The mask melted so closely onto the head that no human could ever tell it wasn't his real face. Acting as Grinsby once more, he backed the truck until it was in front of the Kramar house. He drove it into the driveway and parked, leaving the engine running. He hopped out. Then using a small, warm key with an X on one end and a snake's head on the other, he opened the big garage door. He drove the truck inside the garage and closed the door.

Using the same key, he opened the glove compartment in the truck and took out a small black can. It looked like a can of spray paint. A white circled X was the only label. Grinsby reached back into the glove compartment and brought out a long, sharp hook. The curved end of the hook looked just like a snake's fang.

Using the key, Grinsby let himself into the house. He took the spray can and hook with him. He went straight to the living room.

"Just in time," he said to himself as he looked out the window. The sheriff's car was coming down the street with Mrs. Kramar and the girls. "Might as well take them all." His eyes began to glow red.

He took off the lid of the spray can and pushed the button. A black mist shot out of the can, then dissolved in the air. He filled the room with the mist. Outside, the car doors slammed. Mr. Kramar helped get the bicycles out of the trunk of the car. Susan was the first one to open the front door. Grinsby sat on the couch. With one hand he pulled off the plastic face. The eyes glowed red, the teeth bared in a terrible sort of grin.

Susan smelled something dead the second she opened the door. She stepped inside. The smell was horrible. Her eyes blurred and she felt sick, as if she were going to pass out.

"Mother!" she called out weakiy as she fell to the carpet. She saw something that looked vaguely human sitting on the couch. She wanted to scream, but by then she was too weak. Her eyes closed.

Mrs. Kramar was next in the house. The dead smell was strong. She saw Susan on the floor, but before she could speak, she fell too. Lois and Katherine came in together. They passed out, falling on top of Mrs. Kramar.

Sheriff Kramar walked quickly up the sidewalk. He ran in the open door when he saw everyone lying on the carpet. He didn't have time to speak. His eyes burned, the dead smell suffocating him. He coughed once and fell beside his family.

The creature that had been Grinsby closed the front door. Then he turned to the bodies and held up the fang-shaped hook in front of his face. Two beams of red light shot from his eyes to the hook. In a bright flash, the hook began glowing red, like the creature's eyes. He swung the hook down toward Sheriff Kramar's neck. But a few inches away from the sheriff's throat, the hook hit something invisible that made a metal clanking sound. The creature pulled back on the hook and Sheriff Kramar's body began to slide across the floor. The sound of a heavy, rattling chain filled the room. The creature pulled the sheriff to the truck in the garage. Then he went back for the others.

One by one he dragged the bodies to the waiting black box in the back of his truck. Each time he hooked some invisible link around their necks. The X-Removal Plan was working like a dream.

A VISIT WITH GRANDFATHER KRAMAR

· · · · · · · ·

16

John soared higher and faster on the Spirit Flyer, letting it take him where it wanted to go. He had never flown so far away from the town. Farms and fields passed below him. The clear blue sky felt delicious and crisp. Flying on the old red bike was always fun. But it was even more exciting knowing the bike was taking him on another adventure, to a new place.

The Spirit Flyer had a speed of its own. The wheels turned by themselves while John's feet rested on the pedals. Twice John tried to turn the bike to look at something on the ground more closely, but the bike didn't slow down. John soon realized he should just let the bike take him where it wanted.

He wondered if his aunt and uncle were worrying about him. He didn't know about the unusual things Horace Grinsby was doing at that minute, using a gas that smelled like death, chains you couldn't see and a strange black box.

As John searched the ground trying to recognize places he had visited before, a shadowy cloud appeared in the blue sky just behind him, blowing along at the same speed as John. The cloud swirled, changing into an angry tornado. But then two red eyes appeared, a white circled X and, as the mouth opened, two red fangs. Its tongue flicked out silently. John still did not see it. Then its mouth opened wide and moved closer.

John had been watching the shadow of the Spirit Flyer race down the highway below him. Suddenly he saw a huge shadow overtake the shadow of the Spirit Flyer.

"What's that?" John said, looking closer. The shadow had a strangely familiar shape. It almost looked like a . . .

John turned in his seat. The sky was blotted out with the enormous presence of the serpent, the mouth opened wide, two fangs bigger than telephone poles oozing with poison.

John opened his mouth to scream, but the Spirit Flyer suddenly shot forward. For an instant, John felt a hard wind on his face, then nothing. The ground below was a blur of greens and browns, then a flash of white. He heard a small shrill hum. Then the earth came into focus once more.

"What happened?" John asked, sitting high in the air. He whirled around, expecting to see the gigantic snake. But the sky was an empty blue.

"Where did it go?" he asked himself. "And where am I?"

Then he saw something familiar: a red barn with a big white door next to an old white house with a long picket fence. From high in the air it looked different, but John still recognized it— Grandfather Kramar's farm!

"Boy, that was fast," John said. The trip usually took five hours in the car. But John had flown there in twenty minutes. He looked nervously behind him again, afraid the snake might reappear, but the sky was clear.

Just then, the old red bike began descending to the ground, passing over the large pond used to water the cows. John saw a man with white hair in the alfalfa field next to the workshop. The man was waving at him.

Even from the air, John could see Grandfather Kramar's warm smile. John waved back. The Spirit Flyer glided down and landed gently in the cool alfalfa next to his grandfather.

"That's quite a bicycle, young man," Grandfather Kramar said, his bright eyes twinkling in his old wrinkled face. John jumped off the Spirit Flyer, knocked the kickstand down, then ran to hug his grandfather.

"Aren't you surprised that it flies?" John asked excitedly.

"Well, when you're as old as me you see a lot of strange things over the years if you stay alert," the old man said and smiled. "Like your face. You're awful pale, boy. Looks like you've seen a ghost. And you're trembling."

John looked down at his hands. They *were* shaking. He had moved so fast, he didn't have time to be scared when he saw the snake. Now the fear was coming out.

"Something's after me!" John said. "Something's in the air. And it's terrible . . . it's big, bigger than a tornado. And it looks just like a snake. It has red eyes and red fangs and a white circle with an X inside on its chest. It was behind me, its mouth open. Then something happened and I was here all of a sudden. But I don't see it now. The sky is clear."

A serious look crossed Grandfather Kramar's face. He looked up at the clear blue sky for a moment, then frowned. "Let's go to the shop," the old man said. "We have work to do."

John tried to push the Spirit Flyer through the tall green alfalfa, but the wheels got tangled.

"Here," Grandfather Kramar said, sitting down on the back of the old bike. "Let's ride."

"I don't think it will carry . . ."

But before John finished, the old red bicycle rose into the air and glided over the field to the workshop.

"I've never given anyone a ride before," John said. Grandfather Kramar only smiled. They landed just outside of the workshop's door.

"A real smooth ride," Grandfather Kramar said. "A Spirit Flyer always gives a smooth ride. Even smoother if you know how to sit right on one."

"You've ridden a Spirit Flyer before?" John asked.

"Sure. But first things first," the old man said. He looked up at the sky again. John looked too. But the sky was still clear. Grandfather Kramar shook his head mysteriously. "Let's take it inside for a better look."

John rolled the Spirit Flyer into the workshop. Once inside, he breathed deeply, smelling the aroma of leather, wood and grease; a rich, exciting smell that reminded him of all the happy times he had spent inside the old shop, playing with his cousins or watching his grandfather fix things. John especially liked playing on the old red tractor that was parked inside the shop. He loved to sit in the seat of the tractor, turning the old worn steering wheel, pushing the gears, pretending he was driving. His grandfather had let him steer it many times when they plowed the garden or cut the grass.

"Let's roll it over by the workbench," Grandfather Kramar said, switching on the light. John knocked the kickstand down. Grandfather Kramar ran his experienced hands over the Spirit Flyer as if he were looking for something.

John watched carefully, knowing the wonder of those old hands. He had seen his grandfather fix almost anything. And the toys Grandfather Kramar could build out of scraps of wood, wire and leather were amazing. John had a whole collection of toys in his room, all made by Grandfather Kramar.

Finally, his hands stopped rubbing the old bicycle. Grandfather Kramar stood up. He looked concerned. He walked over to the window and stared into the sky.

"What's wrong?" John asked. He ran over to the window. The sky was still clear and blue. "I don't see it. But the snake was right behind me. Don't you believe me?"

"Of course I believe you," the old man said. "But why don't you tell me everything from start to finish about this bicycle. Where you got it and so on."

The old man walked over to an old white refrigerator and took out two quart jars of ice tea. John licked his lips. Grandfather Kramar always seemed to know what you wanted even before you wanted it. He poured John a glass, and one for himself. John sipped the cool tea and began his story.

Once in a while Grandfather Kramar asked a question, but most of the time he just listened, whittling a piece of wood with a pocketknife. John drank three glasses of tea while telling the story of the junk yard, how he discovered the bike flew, how it stopped flying, how the bikes were stolen and how they were found.

Grandfather Kramar smiled. He sliced off a few more pieces of wood, then looked at what he was making. He turned it over in his hands.

"Uncle Bill and Aunt Betty said you might know something about why all these things happened," John said. Then he added softly, "Maybe that you would tell me something about my father and mother. I don't understand anything. But since we got the thieves, I guess it's all over now."

Grandfather Kramar looked up quickly. He stared at John.

"It's not over," the old man said solemnly. "It's not over at all. The thieves stealing the bicycles was just another trick to get the Spirit Flyer away from you. The snake is what matters, and you said the snake was right behind you before you came here."

"Well, the sky is clear now," John said.

"No, it isn't clear," the old man said, his face serious. "There's something in the air. And in a few minutes you'll see it. But first things first."

Grandfather Kramar put down the piece of wood and pocketknife. He opened a cabinet drawer and took out a small bottle with a cork. After pulling out the cork, he poured a clear liquid from the bottle onto a rag. The liquid had an odd smell.

"What's that?" John asked.

"It's something that will make things clear," Grandfather Kramar said, as he squatted down beside the Spirit Flyer. Right below where the handlebars connected to the frame, Grandfather Kramar rubbed with the rag. The red paint started to dissolve.

"I don't think I sanded it there or even painted because it wasn't rusty," John said.

"Of course it wasn't rusty," Grandfather Kramar said. He stood up. "Look."

The old man pointed to the place where he had dissolved the paint.

John bent over. What he saw made him feel calm and quiet inside, yet he wasn't sure why. He dropped down to his knees and just stared. Three small golden crowns connected to each other were stuck into the metal right below the handlebars. A chill passed through John's body like deep music. He touched the crowns with his finger. They were made of real metal, not paint or a decal.

"They were carefully hidden in thick paint," Grandfather Kramar said. "You weren't supposed to see them, just like you weren't supposed to take this bicycle home and fix it. That snake was there to scare you away, just like the one that followed you here. In fact, it's outside now, waiting."

"What?" John said, jumping to his feet.

"Now stay calm," Grandfather Kramar said. "That's why I showed you the crowns first. This is a genuine Spirit Flyer. One has to be certain since there are fakes. We are safe. This bicycle comes from the Three Kings."

"The Three Kings?" John asked. "What kings? Where are they? Who are they?"

Grandfather Kramar smiled. He squeezed the boy's shoulder, then walked over to the old red tractor. From under the seat he pulled out a pair of goggles, such as an old-time airplane pilot would wear. The same sign of the Three Crowns was stuck into the frame right between the two eyepieces. In tiny letters on both sides was the name: "Spirit Flyer Vision."

"You mean these kings make more than bicycles?" John asked.

"Yes," the old man said. "Let's go to the window."

"But you said that big snake was out there," John said, pulling back on his hand.

"Do you want to know the answers to your questions or don't you?" Grandfather Kramar asked patiently. "Many times we ask questions we don't really want answered."

"I want to know," John said, looking fearfully at the window. "At least I think I do."

"Yes or no?" Grandfather Kramar said. "Maybe you're not ready yet. Maybe you're too young still."

"Yes. I want to know," John said, though in his heart he still felt fear.

"Good," Grandfather Kramar said. "You've seen the crowns; now you need to see something in the air."

"I don't see how those crowns answer anything," John said. "And I don't like that snake."

"That's a normal *and* healthy attitude," the old man said. "But we are safe here. Trust me."

Reluctantly, John followed his grandfather over to the window of the workshop. He flattened himself against the wall, then carefully peeked outside. The sky was clear and blue.

"There's nothing there," John said, stepping in front of the window. He looked out. It was a beautiful sunny day.

"Look closer," Grandfather Kramar said. John looked.

"I don't see anything," John said.

"Look at the alfalfa field on the hill," the old man said.

John looked. Everything appeared normal. Just alfalfa.

"But there's nothing there," John said.

"Look deeper," Grandfather Kramar said. "See the darkness?"

"Look deeper?" John asked. "What darkness?"

John looked again. Then he saw what his grandfather meant. Part of the field was darker, covered in a shadow.

"That's only a shadow," John said, beginning to feel impatient. Then it hit him. There was nothing in the sky to make a shadow! John looked at the clear blue sky, then back at the shadow. Ever so slightly the shadow moved. John then recognized the shadow's shape—the shape of the giant snake.

"It's the snake!" John screamed. "He's here. But where is he? What will we do?"

John searched the sky frantically, afraid to see the monstrous snake, but even more scared not seeing it.

"You are only seeing a shadow, John," the old man said patiently. "It's there. In the air. But I want you to look deeper."

"Deeper?" John asked. "How can I look deeper? What do you mean?"

"I will put these goggles on you," Grandfather Kramar said. "I think you will be able to see. These are special goggles, John. And if you do see, you will never in all your life forget what you see. But it's a beginning to the answers of some of your questions. But only a beginning. Maybe you'll understand better why the Spirit Flyer found you and also why . . ."

"But I found the Spirit Flyer," John interrupted. "I found it at the dump, with Roger."

Grandfather Kramar smiled. He patted John's back with his old hands, then squeezed his shoulder.

"You have much to learn," the old man said. "That bicycle is full of more secrets than you can imagine. But that's why we will use the

goggles to see deeper than our imagination allows. Then you can see why things aren't completed. It isn't over. You see only one shadow, that of a horrible snake. But that's only a tiny part of the whole Deeper World."

John stared out the window again. The shadow remained large on the hill of alfalfa. The words of his grandfather puzzled him, yet he felt a certain excitement, as if he almost understood something new and powerful, and even dangerous.

"Now I want you to close your eyes," Grandfather Kramar said. "I will put the goggles on you. But keep your eyes closed. Then when I tell you, I want you to open your eyes, but only for a second. One glance will be enough."

"But I can already see through the goggles," John said, seeing his grandfather's hand behind the dark glass.

"You are only seeing the surface side," the old man said. "But if you look through from the other side, you will see deeper. Now close your eyes."

John squeezed his eyes shut. The old rubber strap of the goggles pinched his ears and pulled his hair. Then they rested on his nose. Grandfather Kramar held his shoulders and pointed him so he was looking out the window.

"Why are you holding onto me?" John asked.

"For safety," the old man answered. "Do you feel ready?"

"Yes."

"Ok. Open your eyes. Look deeper."

John opened his eyes. Almost as soon as his eyes were open, he began to scream, but only a small sound came out of his mouth, as if he were breathless. His body went stiff, then suddenly fell back limp into Grandfather Kramar's waiting arms.

The boy had fainted at his vision of the Deeper World.

THE DEEPER WORLD
· · · · · · · · ·
17

Grandfather Kramar laid John on the floor. He carefully took off the Spirit Flyer Vision goggles and put them away under the tractor seat. Then he slowly whittled the piece of wood with his pocketknife, waiting for John to wake up.

In a few minutes, John opened his eyes, looking somewhat confused and slightly afraid.

"Where am I?" he asked.

"With us," Grandfather Kramar said, reaching down to give John a hand. "Why don't you have a sip of tea?"

John walked over to the workbench, drank a whole glass of tea in one breath, then walked cautiously to the window. He stared at the long shadow on the hill of alfalfa, then looked into the sky, the seemingly empty blue sky.

"What is it, Grandfather?" John asked softly, still staring at the sky, a sky that would never be the same.

"Of course I'm sure you only saw a small part," Grandfather Kramar said. "But what you saw was a glimpse of the Deeper World."

"The Deeper World," John repeated in a whisper. "A glimpse is enough. But it seemed so long, like hours . . . though I knew it was only a second, yet . . . I can't explain. It was, . . . it was . . ."

The old man nodded sympathetically. He patted John on the back.

"One can't look at the Deeper World too long," Grandfather Kramar said. "Not unless you are protected. It's like looking at the sun; it's both too bright *and* too dark. Too strong for our human eyes."

"But what is it, this Deeper World?" the boy asked.

"I can't really describe it in words," the old man said. "It's beyond what any human language allows, though once in a while a poet will give it a good try. But if you knew the language of angels and the secrets of dreams, you would begin to know the Deeper World. We can't touch dreams, yet dreams touch us, making us feel sad or happy or afraid. The Deeper World is something like that, but much, much more: a dimension beyond us, yet in us too. The Deeper World is like an invisible world that holds our world together; it touches our flesh and bones, as well as our thoughts and dreams. That's why it seemed so long when you saw it, even though it was only a second in our time. It was as if you saw a glimpse of eternity through a crack between times."

"But it wasn't just the time, Grandfather," John said. "I saw *things*. Not just that snake but other things. Yet some had those white-circled Xs and others had the sign of the Three Crowns. And then that snake. Only it was different. I could see things inside it, and it went on and on like a dark tunnel without an end. Oh, Grandfather. I don't like the Deeper World. It's full of monsters and horrible things, and they're all invisible!"

"They aren't really invisible in the way you think, but deeper," Grandfather Kramar said. "The air we breathe is invisible, but it isn't deeper."

"But what are those . . . things?" John asked, pointing at the sky which had always seemed so empty before. "Why are so many of them hanging around here? I couldn't have counted them if I tried. They scare me."

"Those things you saw are a type of being that lives in the Deeper World," the old man said. "And you aren't the first person to be scared at their sight. They are called the Aggeloi."

"The what?"

"The Aggeloi," Grandfather Kramar said. "Only some of them aren't true Aggeloi anymore. The ones with the circled X are dead Aggeloi, called Daimones. The sign of the circled X is a sign of death."

"They didn't look dead to me," John said, glancing at the window. "They were moving. So was the snake."

"Death is not always what we think it is," the old man said. "There are many ways to be dead and many ways to cause death. Just because something or someone exists doesn't mean they have the Magic of life. The Daimones are death rebels."

"But why are there so many around here?" John asked. "It's like they are watching me."

"They *are* watching you," Grandfather Kramar said.

"What?"

"Don't get excited," the old man said. "Let me tell you a short story, though it might sound a little odd at first. A long time ago, Magic filled the Deeper World and our world. Three Magical Kings ruled over all. Deep peace was in every heart. But then a powerful prince of the Aggeloi wanted more power and defied the kings, wishing to kill them. This Aggelo called himself Treason. Because he broke the Deeper Laws of the Kingdom of the Kings, his Magic died. Yet his deeper powers remained. But deeper powers without Magic are Tragic. Other Aggeloi broke the Deeper Laws and followed Treason, becoming his slaves. A war started. Treason and his army of dead Aggeloi, the Daimones, fought against the Kingdom of the Kings.

"To stop Treason and his rebels of death, the kings held a trial on a lesser world. Treason fought hard. He made slaves of anyone who chose Tragic powers instead of Magic, putting them into Deeper Chains. For a time, Magic was all but lost on the lesser world. But then one of the kings, the King Prince, came to the lesser world to prove that Magic was stronger than the powers of Tragic. Magic returned with him to the lesser world for those who wished to be in the Kingdom of the Kings. The King Prince left to prepare a new Magic place in the Kingdom. When he returns he will put Treason and all his followers in a Deep Dungeon. But until then, Treason still exists to increase death, trying to stop all Magic, like you and your bicycle. That's why they are around this house watching you. The Aggeloi wish you Magic. The Daimones wish you Tragic."

"But why me?" John asked. "I'm just a boy."

"That doesn't matter," Grandfather Kramar said. "A child, especially a child with a Spirit Flyer, is a great threat to the Daimones."

"But why?"

"Because you still have the ability to wish and believe in Magic," the old man said. "The Daimones hate Magic. They want you to be their slave, locked in their chains."

"I did see chains," the boy said, remembering his vision through the goggles. "Huge, dark chains. And somehow they were all connected. Only some weren't connected too."

"Some chains are broken," Grandfather Kramar said. "That's why the Daimones are afraid of you. You have the Spirit Flyer and might break more chains. You must be interfering with one of their plans. The giant snake is made of the dark shadows of death to scare you and keep you from flying the Spirit Flyer."

"The snake is made of shadows?" John asked. "You mean it's not real?"

"Of course it's real," the old man said. "As real as shadows, lies and fears. Only these are Deeper Shadows. Shadows so strong you can touch the darkness as if it were hard, like brick. And it can touch you."

"Grandfather, I don't like this," John said, feeling the fear touch him like a hand in a soft black glove. "And I'm not sure I really understand."

"Well, it's time you learned more of the secrets of that Magic bicycle, boy," Grandfather Kramar said. "Let's go over to the tractor. I want you to sit in the seat and listen to the story of Magic. Then maybe you'll understand more about the Spirit Flyer, the giant snake and the rest of the Deeper World."

John sat down in the worn seat of the old red tractor. Grandfather Kramar pulled out an old leather aviator's cap, the kind with earflaps. The sign of the Three Crowns was in the center of the cap on the front. John felt a chill pass through his body when he saw the golden shine. On the edge of the cap were the words, "Spirit Flyer Headgear." A red wire ran from the back of the cap into the body of the tractor right below the speedometer. Next to the wire was a single red button.

"Put on the cap," Grandfather Kramar said. "And close your eyes."

"It doesn't fit very well," John said. "It's too big."

"Well, you're young," Grandfather Kramar said. "Sometimes you have to grow to fit the story. But what you lack in headsize will be made up in the size of your wishes. When you're ready, push that red starter button. It will start you thinking of the Deeper World."

"Will it hurt?" John asked. "Will it be like those goggles?"

"Well, it will only hurt if you don't want to listen," the old man said. "The goggles are much stronger. The headgear will tell you the story of Magic, but in the time of the Deeper World—like the wink of an eye—because our time is short right now."

The boy put his finger on the red button, then closed his eyes.

"Ok," he said. "I'm ready, I guess."

"Then push the button."

John pushed the button. If you had stood next to him, you would have heard only a single, deep note of music.

The boy smiled, then opened his eyes.

"Wow, that's some story," John said. Then his face became serious. "But Grandfather, will those Daimones try to kill me? I mean, if the Prince, the Kingson, hasn't returned yet, and their powers are stronger near the end, what do I do?"

"Listen," the old man said, holding the boy's shoulders in his large hands. "There are many mysteries of the Deeper World that I do not yet understand, and I am an old man. But I do know this: you are safe when you are on the Spirit Flyer. It is your gift of Magic from the kings. Never give up that Magic. Hold on tight to the handlebars, and you will always arrive where you need to go. Sometimes that old red bike may take you to strange places, places where you may be afraid. But never let go. Even if your hands are weak, it will hold onto you as long as you wish, deep in your heart, for the Magic. The Aggeloi too will protect you. They have already protected you. When the snake spit lightning at you and the bike jumped out of the way, that was the Aggeloi. They moved you."

"Really?" John asked.

"The snake was trying to scare you off," Grandfather Kramar said. "He wanted you to be so afraid that you would lose faith in the Spirit Flyer and jump. Since you already *have* a Spirit Flyer, they have lost one battle. So now they are trying to stop you from riding it."

"I wish Uncle Bill believed what I told him about the Spirit Flyer," John said. "But I didn't know about the kings or the Daimones then."

"I think he does believe you," Grandfather Kramar said, "even though he wants to believe his laws and rules explain everything. But more than that, your uncle is in a shadow of fear, and he has believed the lies of that deadly fear because of what happened to your father and mother, John."

"But if they died in a car accident, why would Uncle Bill be afraid of my Spirit Flyer?" John asked. "I don't understand. It seemed like Uncle Bill didn't even want me to talk about the Spirit Flyer."

"Do you know what kind of work your father did, John?" the old man asked.

"He was a schoolteacher."

"Yes, for a while," Grandfather Kramar said. "He taught sixth grade. He was a good teacher too. But he stopped teaching and opened a store. A toy store."

"A toy store? I didn't know that."

"Well, he didn't have it long. He sold toys from various companies, but he also made toys. He wished deeply to give children joy through the Magic of toys. Then one day two bicycles were left outside his workshop door. Those bicycles were Spirit Flyers from the Three Kings."

John's mouth dropped open.

"Your father quickly discovered the unusual abilities of those bicycles," Grandfather Kramar said. "And one day he and your mother rode them up here. Took them about an hour."

"You mean they flew too?" John asked. "So that's why you weren't surprised to see me. Uncle Bill and Aunt Betty must have known about the Spirit Flyers then."

"Well, your father tried to tell them, but Bill wouldn't believe it," the old man said. "There aren't rules in his books about flying bicycles. Your father tried to show Bill, but Bill wasn't ready to see. Your father became impatient, then angry. Getting angry was a mistake because then the bikes wouldn't fly. The Magic can't work. Then the long rain came."

"The long rain?" John asked.

"A long, unusual rain poured on Centerville for several days," Grandfather Kramar said. "No one had seen a rain like it before. Other towns near Centerville didn't get a drop. But Centerville flooded. And people saw clouds, like funnel clouds. But your father and mother saw something deeper—a funnel cloud that was really a snake. A snake that spit lightning, a snake that bit trees into pieces. Your father tried to tell Bill. But Bill wouldn't believe him any more about the snake than he would about the Spirit Flyer's being able to fly. Then, a few days later, they found your parents' car smashed up, as if a tornado had twisted it like a tin can."

John sighed. Even though he could barely remember his parents, he still missed them in quiet ways.

"Your parents were assumed to be dead," the old man said. "But there was a mystery. Only their car was found. No one ever found your parents. And besides that, the two Spirit Flyer bicycles also disappeared. No one knows why. I even searched for your parents on my Spirit Flyer, but I didn't find them."

"You have a bicycle too?" John asked.

"No, no," Grandfather Kramar said and smiled. He patted the old red tractor, then pointed at the side. In flowing white letters inside a white border was the proud name, "Spirit Flyer Harvester."

"I never even noticed that you had a . . ."

John stopped. His eyes were fixed on the old crank telephone on the wall by the refrigerator.

"L-l-look!" John stuttered, pointing at the telephone. Grandfather Kramar turned. The old phone was glowing, blinking on and off like a taillight. The old man just stared for a moment, then shook his head.

"Don't be afraid," he said. "Looks like we're going to get a little call."

"But that phone isn't even hooked up to anything," John said.

"Well, it appears as if something from the Deeper World is hooked up to it," Grandfather Kramar replied. He walked over to the phone and took it off the hook. Even he was surprised to hear the voice of Susan screaming.

"John, John, oh, John. Come get us. It has us. It's so awful and dark. He wants to . . ."

A tremendous scream drowned out her words. As the scream died away, a terrible hissing noise drifted out of the phone. Then it was the same dark voice John had heard the night before.

"We want you, John Kramar. Go home now if you want to see your family alive again. We have them all this time. Remember your parents. Don't refuse us. We have them all."

FIGHTING TRAGIC WITH MAGIC

• • • • • • • •

18

The phone stopped glowing. Grandfather Kramar hung it up, but John just kept staring as if frozen by the voice.

"I don't like this . . . Deeper World, Grandfather," the boy said.

"I hoped we would have more time," Grandfather Kramar said slowly. "But I guess not. You need to be prepared."

"I'm going right now," John said, as if breaking out of a trance.

"Wait just a second," the old man said. He knew how hard the shadow had fallen on the boy. "Don't go rushing off trying to be a hero."

"But they have Susan!" John yelled. "And she said all my family. I've already lost my parents to . . . to something in . . ."

"Don't raise your voice to me, boy," Grandfather Kramar said firmly. "You don't know what's been lost or gained in this situation or that of your parents."

John started to snap back at his grandfather but stopped. "I'm sorry," John said. "But shouldn't I go save them?"

"Save them?" Grandfather Kramar asked. "How can you save them? You don't even know where they are or what to save them from. That might not have been Susan's voice but a fake. Be careful of lies."

"But how can I tell the difference?" John asked, more frustrated than ever.

"That's why I'm telling you to be prepared," the old man said. "I want you to go sit down on the Spirit Flyer right now."

"But shouldn't I *try* to save her?" John insisted.

"No," Grandfather Kramar said, much to John's surprise. "Your only hope is to stay with the Spirit Flyer. If the Daimones have her, what can you do? How can you fight them? You can't see them. And when you did see them with the goggles, you fainted. You can't fight the battles of the Deeper World with the weapons of our lesser world. You need Magic to stop Tragic."

John looked down. He made his hands into fists, then realized the uselessness of his own hands. He walked over to the old red bicycle and sat down. Finally, he was ready to listen.

"What should I do?" the boy asked.

"Ride the Spirit Flyer where it takes you," Grandfather Kramar said. "But first, put on the instruments that came with it."

"The what?"

"Didn't it have things like a light, a horn, a mirror—things like that?"

"Yes," John replied. "But they were all broken, so I took them off. I have them in a box in the garage."

"Well, go home and put them back on," the old man said. "Your Spirit Flyer isn't complete without them. And I also want you to take something else."

The old man went over to his workbench and opened a drawer. He brought back a wooden object.

"It's a slingshot," John said. The sign of the Three Crowns was burned into the wood. "But it doesn't have the rubber bands or the pouch."

The old man nodded. He got a pair of scissors, then went over to the tractor. John couldn't see what his grandfather cut, but in a moment he returned with a small piece of leather.

"What about the rubber bands?" John asked.

"You must put them on yourself," the old man replied. "Use the old inner tubes you took off the Spirit Flyer."

"How did you know I kept the inner tubes?" John asked.

"I just knew," Grandfather Kramar replied with a smile.

"But it's just a slingshot," John protested. "How can this help me?"

"It's made of a special wood," Grandfather replied. "And it carries the mark of the Three Kings. Remember it's not the object but the power behind the object."

"I still don't see how this stuff can help," John complained. "I mean, you said I can't fight them."

"You are not going to fight but to rescue," the old man said. "If they really have Susan and the others, all you need is to rescue them. Escape is victory. Staying on the Spirit Flyer is victory. Don't try to fight. That is their trick to separate you from Magic."

John shook his head. He looked at the slingshot, then reluctantly put it in his pocket.

"I just don't understand," the boy said.

"We can't always wait until we understand, especially the ways of the Deeper World," Grandfather Kramar said. "But the more you ride that old bike, the more you will learn. It takes Magic. I couldn't explain the Deeper World. You had to see it through the goggles."

"Yes, but . . ."

"And I can't explain the realm of the dead," Grandfather Kramar said. "But they are powerful. A dead snake can still bite and the poison will kill. But stay on the Spirit Flyer. The kings have provided all the Magic you need. You only have to hold onto the handlebars. Obey that much and the rest is given."

John looked out the window and saw the snake's shadow waiting on the hill of alfalfa.

"Should I go now?" John asked.

"Yes," the old man said. "Just stay on the Spirit Flyer. You are seated on Magic; the snake cannot harm you there."

The old man opened the workshop door. He too saw the long shadow waiting. John rolled the old red bicycle to the door, took a deep breath, then got on.

The Spirit Flyer rolled forward immediately, gliding up into the clear blue sky, turning toward Centerville. As John passed over the workshop roof, Grandfather Kramar called to him.

"Hold on tight," the old man shouted. "Never let go."

John nodded and turned to face the open sky. Grandfather Kramar watched until the boy and bicycle were out of sight.

As the old man walked back to the workshop, he looked out at the alfalfa field. The long shadow was gone too.

INTO THE
MOUTH OF
DARKNESS

19

John's mind raced with questions almost as fast as the Spirit Flyer soared through the air. The old red bike chose its own speed. John held on firmly to the handlebars, his feet resting on the pedals.

Suddenly, without warning, the Spirit Flyer shot ahead faster. John heard a high-pitched hum, and a blur of colors flashed before his eyes. Then everything was the same as before. He was still riding high in the air but the scenery had changed. The sky above him was covered with gray rain clouds, and Centerville was just ahead. The Spirit Flyer had carried the boy two hundred fifty miles in the blink of an eye.

John was surprised, but he let the old red bike choose its own way. At the edge of town, the bike glided down to the street for a smooth landing. John wanted to pedal to the sheriff's office, but since the Spirit Flyer kept moving by itself, he decided to just keep riding. A few minutes later the old red bike rolled up the driveway of the Kramar house and stopped at the garage door.

John hopped off to open the door. The bike rolled into the garage by itself, stopping in front of the tall metal shelves. Outside, rain began to fall in a miserable drizzle: the same kind of rain that had caused the floods. John looked at the rain and felt a stab of fear.

And from that fear, more fear flooded into him. In fact, as soon as he had gotten off the Spirit Flyer, he began to worry about Susan and the family. John looked up at the cardboard box filled with the old broken bicycle instruments and remembered what his grandfather said.

"I'd better see who's home first," he said softly, then ran into the house.

"Uncle Bill! Aunt Betty! They have Susan and maybe . . ."

But the boy stopped, feeling the eerie silence and smelling a strange smell, the smell of something dead. The whole house seemed as if it had been abandoned for months. John ran from room to room, only to find the next room more empty than the one before it.

The phone in the kitchen was off the hook, dangling lifelessly on the cord. John started to put it on the hook when suddenly the phone screamed and began to glow.

"Help us, John. . . . They have us all! Dad, Mom and the girls. You must save us. Come quick, right away. To the old dump. John, we need . . ." But Susan's words were drowned out in a horrible scream.

John dropped the glowing phone as if it were on fire. It swayed in the dead silence.

The boy sat down at the kitchen table. His heart pounded and his legs felt weak, as if he couldn't stand. He was so afraid he couldn't think. Too much was happening. The Deeper World . . . Daimones . . . the dead smell in the empty house. His mind blurred. The loneliness of the house filled him.

Then John saw the note lying on the kitchen table, written in slashes of thick red ink.

To John Kramar:

Into the mouth
of darkness fly
above the clouds
above the sky,
Two red fangs
and two red eyes.
Come in quickly
or they all will die.

John read the note again. What could it mean? Susan had said to go to the old dump. Was that a trick? Her voice sounded so real, it must have been Susan, the boy thought. But what did Grandfather Kramar say? Put on those old instruments that he had taken off the Spirit Flyer? In his fear, the boy had almost forgotten.

"I must save them," John said. He ran out to the garage. The Spirit Flyer was leaning against the metal shelves. John reached high and grabbed the cardboard box. The old broken light, the cracked mirror, the gear lever, the old rubber horn, and the generator were all still there, along with the old black inner tubes.

The slingshot, John thought. Using heavy scissors, he quickly cut two long strips of rubber from one of the inner tubes. He tied the ends to the slingshot. Then he tied the bands to the leather pouch; the slingshot was ready.

"But what about rocks or bullets or something for the slingshot?" John asked. "Grandpa didn't give me anything to shoot. What good is an empty slingshot with those . . . creatures? Or even people?"

John threw the slingshot down on the workbench in disgust. He stared at all the old instruments in the box.

"They're broken and useless," the boy said. "Grandpa must have thought they were in better shape. And I don't have time. Susan said come right away."

John had an idea. He suddenly ran back into the house to his aunt and uncle's bedroom. He saw it on the top of the dresser— the gun his uncle used as sheriff. The revolver weighed more than he remembered, but he quickly strapped it around his waist. Outside, a brilliant flash split the sky, followed by a clap of thunder. The rain came down harder.

John ran through the house back into the garage. He felt stronger with the gun on his hip, like a Western gunfighter. He hopped on the Spirit Flyer and pushed with his foot, but the bike wouldn't roll. He pushed harder.

"Come on," John said. "We don't have much time."

But the old red bike wouldn't budge. For an instant, John thought of riding Susan's bike to the dump. He pushed once more with his foot. The Spirit Flyer seemed glued to the ground. He knew the bike wasn't moving for a reason, yet he was too scared and in too much of a hurry to try to understand why. He pushed again, but nothing happened.

"What's wrong?" John asked impatiently.

At that moment he saw the slingshot lying on the workbench. He looked at the sign of the Three Crowns burned into the handle.

"Ok, I'll take it," he said, as if answering someone. He grabbed the slingshot and hung it on the handlebars. Then he noticed the cardboard box with the bicycle instruments." I don't have time to put them on. Besides, they're broken. I've got Uncle Bill's gun."

John pushed with his foot and the old red bike finally moved forward, but very slowly as if it were stuck in a puddle of gooey tar. He looked back at the cardboard box. The old broken instruments seemed to beg to be put on the bicycle, yet John kept pushing until he reached the garage door. "I just don't have time," he said, pushing so hard his leg ached.

At that moment, the old red bike rolled easily out into the driveway.

"Good," John said, feeling a tinge of guilt. Then he looked up and saw the angry black clouds and the ugly rain. His fears returned. The day almost seemed like night, it was so dark.

Then somewhere, far away, lost out in the rain, John thought he heard someone call his name. But who could be calling him? The voice sounded odd. Then it was gone. Lightning flashed, followed by thunder. John shivered. His pajamas were getting wet.

"I should have changed into regular clothes," he said. But before he could go back inside, the Spirit Flyer rolled down the driveway, taking off into the air before it reached the street. John forgot about his wet pajamas and held on. The old red bike gained speed, flying higher over the quiet streets of Centerville. The rain seemed heavy, as if it forced the bike to go slower. But on the outside of town, as it passed over the Sleepy Eye River, the bike sped up, turning in the direction of the old dump.

John felt better when the bike went faster. But at that moment he heard a terrible roar, and a brilliant flash blinded his eyes. The bike jerked to one side. The air smelled of hot electricity—lightning! Far below, an old dead tree began to burn. John shivered. The lightning had just missed him.

Then he was jerked to the other side as another bolt shot by an instant later with a tremendous boom. The flash of light was so strong that John couldn't see for a few seconds, though it seemed longer. He held on blindly to the handlebars.

The old red bike picked up speed, racing toward the dump in the increasing rain. John held on tightly. Then straight ahead, through the hard rain, John saw the source of the lightning. Two large red eyes stared out of the black clouds. But one cloud was darker and swirled like a tornado. John knew it wasn't a cloud at all. As he raced closer, the snake became clearer, taller than a skyscraper as it hovered over the old dump.

John pushed back on the brake of the Spirit Flyer. The snake opened its terrible mouth; the red fangs glistened like wet blood. A flash leaped from the snake's mouth. John closed his eyes, gripping the handlebars. The old red bike jumped straight up as the thunderous roar of lightning passed beneath his feet. The boy felt the heat through his slippers.

Yet the Spirit Flyer kept moving forward. John opened his eyes. The snake was gone! He blinked and looked again but only saw dark clouds. He was exactly over the old dump.

Then he heard it. High above him, lost in the clouds, a tiny distant voice called his name.

"Johnnnnnn . . . Johnnnnnn . . ." The voice died away.

The Spirit Flyer suddenly tilted up and sped straight for the dark angry clouds. As the bike entered the clouds, the boy was blinded by the mists. Again he heard someone call his name twice. The voice was higher, far above him.

Just before he broke through the clouds, John finally realized what was happening. This was just like his dream. Only this time he wasn't safe in his bed. As he burst through into the brilliant blue sky above the clouds, far off to his right he saw it—coiled and waiting in terrible splendor, the large tornado snake. The white circled X gleamed on its black throat, and its mouth was open wide.

John automatically pushed back on the brake, but the Spirit Flyer raced toward the mountainous serpent.

"Johnnnnnn . . ." the tiny voice called; only this time it was louder. Then to his horror John realized the voice was coming from inside the serpent. The large red eyes glared at him; the red fangs oozed blood. John remembered the note on the kitchen table.

Into the mouth
of darkness fly . . .

A flash of lightning streaked from the dark mouth. But the lightning passed to John's left. Again the snake, like a legless dragon, spit fire. The lightning sizzled to the boy's right. The snake was teasing him. Another bolt flashed over his head.

The Spirit Flyer sped faster toward the waiting mouth of the snake. And as the bike got closer, John began to realize how gigantic the serpent really was. The sky disappeared in unimaginable darkness as the mouth stretched wider and wider.

John pushed back on the brake several times, but the old red bike only went faster toward the giant hole of a mouth. The wheels of the Spirit Flyer weren't even turning anymore; the giant serpent was sucking him into the deeper darkness. John felt powerless. A loud, hissing noise hurt his ears. High above him, he saw the evil point of a red glistening fang coming down toward him—the mouth was closing! The bike was sucked in deeper. The boy looked back and saw the beautiful blue sky disappearing.

Then the mouth shut on a cold, terrible darkness. The deeper darkness, in the realm of increasing death, passed right into the boy like a chilled breath. He felt suffocated. He coughed, trying to free himself, but the darkness increased. He thought the bike was still flying forward, but he wasn't sure. He wasn't even sure his eyes were open. Yet, he felt things pass by him. Weightless whispers of things seemed to touch him.

John gripped the handlebars of the Spirit Flyer tighter. The throbbing, hissing noise became louder and louder as John went deeper. He wanted to cover his ears, but he was afraid to let go of the handlebars.

And as he went even deeper, he began to smell a horrible dead smell—the breath of the serpent: the same dead smell that was in his uncle's house and at the dump the day he had found the Spirit Flyer.

John flew deeper. The noise increased, as did the smell of death and the terrible cold darkness. The boy tried to scream, but his breath was sucked from his mouth, deeper into the darkness.

"I'm going to die," John thought. "There's no air here. I can't breathe. I'm going to die."

The old bike kept speeding forward through the black hole of death, to a world of rotting graves. The darkness seemed to be sucking all the life from the boy's body. The noise was deafening.

"Noooooooo!" John screamed finally.

Then it was over. John felt air rush into his lungs. The noise was gone. The Spirit Flyer had stopped. John put his foot down. The ground, or whatever it was, seemed soft like a sponge, yet firm underneath.

The boy took several deep breaths. When he looked down, he noticed that he could see once again but barely. A cool blue light made his hands look pale, dead.

The light came from a thin crack in the darkness. As John moved closer, he saw that the crack was at the bottom of a door.

"Johnnnnnn . . ." a voice called out weakly from the other side of the door.

THE CENTERVILLE BUREAU OF CHILDREN AND PARENT RELATIONS

20

With a gentle bump from the front wheel of the Spirit Flyer, the door swung slowly open. John held on tightly to the handlebars as the old bike rolled through the doorway.

A wall of blue flame stopped him. The flame seemed cold and poisonous, as if anything it touched would freeze and die.

John looked back to make sure of his way of escape, but the door had disappeared. He looked all around—the wall of flame had surrounded him. He was trapped. Then the circle of fire squeezed closer. John held on. He wanted to run away, but there was no place to run.

"Johnnnnnn . . ." the voice called from beyond the flames.

The fire moved closer and closer. John felt colder, not hotter. He looked around frantically. Just as the flames were about to touch the bike, they split apart. The old red bike rolled through the open passage. Then the flames closed back instantly.

John seemed to be in a large, flat, bare place that stretched out into darkness in all directions, except for the wall of blue flame behind him. Then he saw a tiny desk far ahead of him where the darkness deepened. Someone or something little was sitting at the desk.

The Spirit Flyer rolled quietly and quickly toward the distant desk. As John got closer, he realized that the desk and person weren't tiny at all, but gigantic. John could barely see the top of the person's head over the back of the chair. The person sitting in the chair had his back to the boy and bicycle with the desk in front of him.

Quietly, John pulled his uncle's gun out of the holster. He aimed it at the person.

"This is the Centerville Bureau of Children and Parent Relations," the person said in a familiar voice. "Your little law-keeping device is worthless here, so quit playing good guys and bad guys."

The Spirit Flyer rolled around to the front of the giant desk. John lowered the gun to his side when he saw the figure's face.

"Hello, Dumper," the figure said, laughing. There was no mistake; it was Barry Smedlowe's laugh. And it was Barry Smedlowe's face, only different. Besides being huge, the face was too pale, and the eyes were dull and lifeless like a snake's eyes. Suddenly the eyes glowed solid red. The Barry figure laughed again, yet it did not smile. The face barely moved at all, as if it were a mask of Barry's face on another body. John couldn't see flesh anywhere. The figure wore a strange gray uniform which covered the neck. Black gloves hid the hands. The sign of the circled X was in the center of the chest.

John stared into the lifeless red eyes. "I could kill you," John said defiantly. Whatever it was, it had Barry's personality.

The giant figure roared in laughter, yet the face remained motionless.

The dull red eyes glowed. "You stupid claybrain," the Barry figure answered. "You can't kill what's already dead." The boyish voice seemed wrong for the huge person.

"Are you a Daimone?" John asked. "You look like Barry Smedlowe, but you can't be Barry."

"Who are you to tell me what I am or what I am not?" the Barry figure scoffed. "Barry and I are very, very close. He's my assignment, rather like homework. He's a wonderful learner and such an idiot. The little fool feeds me well. I would hate to lose him."

For a moment there was silence. Then the Barry figure opened his mouth, an endless dark hole with no sign of teeth or tongue. Out of that darkness a red flash streaked like lightning, hitting the gun barrel. The gun glowed red, then drooped like a melted wax candle.

The giant laughed again. The gun felt freezing cold. John dropped it. He stooped down and carefully picked it up. With a sigh, he put it into the holster.

"That gun is garbage here, just like you and that dump-heap bicycle," the Barry figure said. "Garbage waiting to be burned into ashes, Dumper. That's what you'll be."

A noise in the darkness startled John. He turned part way around. Walking out of the darkness into the dim blue light was another gigantic figure in the same kind of gray uniform. The eyes glowed dull red.

But even with those dull red eyes, the figure looked like Doug Barns, one of the Cobra Club members. Though he wasn't as large as the giant, he was still huge. He held a pale blue bowl in his black-gloved hands.

"Doug?" John asked. But the figure ignored him.

"What do you have, slave?" the Barry figure demanded.

"More food has come in, sir," the Doug figure said. His voice sounded like Doug's.

John stood on the pedals on tiptoe to see into the bowl. A large black snake wriggled in a circle. Rearing up, it bared its teeth at the giant.

With his right hand, the Barry figure reached down and grabbed the snake's head. The snake hissed angrily, then bit the black-gloved hand. But the moment the fangs sank into the hand, the snake froze, then crumbled into a pile of ashes. The Barry figure scooped ashes into his mouth. After three handfuls, the bowl was empty. The Doug figure walked back into the darkness, carrying the bowl.

"What was that?" John asked.

"You should know about those snakes," the Barry figure said. "You've made many. You even saw one. I'm told your skid-mark snake was delicious. Death feeds the dead."

The giant laughed without expression.

"Get off that garbage-heap bike!" he commanded.

"No!" John remembered the warnings of his grandfather. He gripped the handlebars more tightly.

"I see you want to suffer," the Barry figure said. "Bring them!"

Out of the darkness, John saw them coming. Katherine was first, followed by Lois, then Susan, then Aunt Betty and finally Uncle Bill. They walked slowly. Then John saw the heavy dark chains around their necks. The whole family was chained together. The neck rings on Katherine and Lois were large for their small throats. The ones on Uncle Bill and Aunt Betty fit tight. The family shuffled closer, their eyes closed as if they were asleep. Yet their eyes seemed forced shut. They were dressed in the same clothes John had seen on them when he left Centerville that morning. Bringing back those stolen bicycles seemed ages ago.

"Uncle Bill? Aunt Betty?" John asked. "Susan, can you hear me?"

"They can't respond, Dumper," the Barry figure said. "They are X-Removed. We X-Removed them in their dreams. It's the same dream. Now they are in our control. They have always been in our control, the same as you. Speak, girl!"

"Johnnnnn . . . oh, Johnnnnn," Susan screamed. "They have us all. Save us. We can't get out."

"I'm here, Susan," John said. But neither Susan nor the rest of the family seemed to hear.

"We have them," the giant said again. "Nothing will free them. In fact, we will kill them, turn them to ashes (such delightful food) unless . . ."

"Unless what?" John asked.

"Unless you sign this Deed in your blood," the Barry figure said. From nowhere he held out a thin piece of black paper made of solid ash. It didn't crumble as John took it.

DEED

I, John Kramar, hereby give up the Spirit Flyer to be destroyed. I will never again associate with or wear the sign of the Three Kings. I will proudly wear the mark of the circled X, the sign of Treason, future king of the Deeper World.

Signed _____

"I have the pen and needle ready," the Barry figure said. He held up an odd pen and a sharp, cruel needle. "Sign this and you will be able to return to your life on Tohu-Vabohu, that garbage-heap world. The others will go with you. Sign quickly. Here's the needle. We need only one drop of blood."

The giant howled with laughter. The needle glistened in the cool blue light.

THE SLINGSHOT OF THE KINGS
········

21

John stared at the long, shining needle. His heart pounded.

"And if I don't sign?" John asked, trying to think of some way to escape. The wall of flame still burned, and the darkness seemed endless in all other directions. John knew that more creatures like the Barry behind the desk were hidden in that darkness.

"You will die completely and slowly," the giant figure said. "And so will your pitiful family. Just like your father and mother. They broke the Order of the Chains. We make ashes of anyone who breaks the Order of the Chains."

"The what?" John asked, stalling for time. He reached for the gun in the holster, then remembered that it was useless.

"The Order of the Chains," the Barry figure said. "We are all made to be a part of the same chain, each of us a link. We are connected to each other, don't you see? The Order of the Chains must be complete before Treason rules the Deeper World forever. We will triumph and kill the king."

"That's not true," John said. "The Kingson won back Magic and broke the powers of the chains."

"Who told you that lie?" the giant roared. His eyes glowed brighter. "That's a fairy tale of the kings. Your parents believed the same thing, and look what happened to them. Ashes. They lost pleasures and powers. We can give you anything you want. Just one drop of blood is all we ask. For now."

"What do you mean, for now?" John asked.

"Since you are only a boy, you will need to contribute more when you are older," the Barry figure said. "Sort of like an installment plan. Little by little you give. It doesn't hurt that way."

"But what did my parents do wrong?" John asked, still stalling. He knew Daimones lied.

"Your father was trying to take back the toys," the giant said. "But *we* control the toys in Centerville. Your father wanted to give out more Spirit Flyers and other things from the kings. He wouldn't cooperate with our plan. He did not obey the Order of the Chains. We turn anyone who disobeys the Order into ashes."

"What was the plan for the toys?" John asked. Grandfather Kramar had said something about plans of the Daimones.

"You are boring me, Dumper," the Barry figure said. "I can't believe you clay-heads are so stupid. We only obey the Order here. Our department covers children and parent relations in Centerville. We're a small department, but we follow the Order. Your parents interfered. Now you and your garbage-heap bicycle are interfering. Quit stalling and sign.

We'll give you another bicycle, one that flies better than the Spirit Flyer. Now sign, or you will have the same fate as your mother and father. You want to save your uncle and his family, don't you? Sign, and they will be able to return."

The giant stood up. The needle glistened cruelly in his black-gloved hand. He pointed at the Deed in John's hand.

John looked around desperately. There was no way to escape. Suddenly, in the surrounding darkness, countless red glowing eyes appeared and stared at him.

"The others are hungry," the Barry figure said, then howled with laughter. "Ashes to ashes."

"Help me," John said softly, looking down at the old red bike. Uncle Bill and the family stood in chains, their eyes closed. Then John's eyes fell on the slingshot. He pulled it off the handlebars.

"You must be an incredibly stupid clay-head to think that little thing can help you," the giant said.

"It carries the sign of the Three Kings," John said defiantly.

"The kings' Magic is no good in this place. You are in our world now."

"It's not the object, but the power behind the object," John said weakly, repeating the words of his grandfather.

"You believe that nonsense?" the figure behind the desk asked. "Your parents believed it too. Don't be stupid. Join us. Soon we will rule all the Deeper World. Think of the power that will be yours."

John forced himself not to listen. His hands shook. In the darkness more blank red eyes appeared; the *things* were coming closer. The Barry figure stepped from behind the desk. The needle in his hand glowed red, then grew longer and bigger, changing into a type of sword John had never seen before. The needle-sword looked wickedly sharp.

"Come fight then, you clay-headed chicken," the giant said. His eyes glowed. "Come on, Dumper. Chick, chick, chickie."

John started to hop off the Spirit Flyer but stopped. He remembered that the gigantic figure wasn't really Barry although the voice was exactly the same. John sat back down on the bike.

"What's the matter?" the Barry figure asked. "Did little Dumper chicken out as usual? Or is it your chain that makes you such a weakling?"

John looked down. A cold chill passed through him when he saw a chain around his neck, just like his uncle's chain and the others'. Suddenly he felt weak, as if his arms and legs were made of jelly. He grabbed the handlebars with his left hand; his right hand held the slingshot.

"You are weak," the giant said, his red eyes glowing colder. "That's what it feels like before we kill you and make you into ashes."

John felt as if he might fall off the Spirit Flyer. He slumped forward slowly. But at the moment he felt his weakest, totally confused by the strange heavy chain, the left handgrip began turning, sliding off the handlebars. In a few seconds it was all the way off.

John almost dropped the handgrip, it felt so heavy. Then he saw a light. Inside the handgrip, something was shining. John tipped the handgrip over into his right hand. A clear marble rolled into his palm, clicking as it hit the handle of the slingshot. Its light was dim yet constant and pure. John understood what to do. Although the marble seemed to weigh a hundred pounds, he put it into the pouch of the slingshot.

"What I have comes from the kings," John said. He could only pull the pouch back an inch. The marble glowed more brightly.

The giant Barry made a hideous roar, raising the needle-sword. In the darkness, the dead marched closer. John held the slingshot in front of him, but it was too heavy to aim.

As the giant swung his needle-sword, John let go of the shining marble.

It shot out, trailing a beam of sparkling light. It cut the needle-sword in half, then passed through the circled X on the giant's chest and out his back. It kept going, spreading in the air, cutting a large hole through the wall of blue flame. The path of light was like a road through the darkness and flame as it traveled deeper.

The gigantic figure didn't fall, but froze solid, smoke hissing from the hole in his chest as if lightning had scorched water. Then slowly the hole began to close.

"Escape now," Katherine said in her tiny voice, "before the evil awakes."

John looked at the path of light and realized that he could escape. The old red bike rolled over to the chained family.

"Escape now. Take my hand," Katherine moaned as if locked in a nightmare. Slipping the slingshot over the handlebar, John grabbed her hand. "Quick. The dead are coming."

John looked around. The hole of light in the giant's chest was shrinking faster. Then he noticed the army of dull red eyes approaching out of the darkness. John saw faces. Each one resembled someone he knew in Centerville. First there was Doug Barns, then Robert Smith and Scott Blake, and the other Cobra Club members. Each was a giant and wore a gray uniform. But there weren't just Cobra Club members. John saw other classmates, girls and boys, his friends. Their eyes glowed and their faces were stiff and blank, all masks. They kept coming. John's mouth dropped open when he saw Roger's face come out of the darkness, the dull red eyes staring into nothing. Then John saw a face that almost made him let go of Katherine's hand.

"Quick. We must escape now," the youngest girl said. "Don't waste time looking at the dead."

John glanced at that one face again, then turned to the pathway of light behind the giant Barry. He still held Katherine's tiny hand in his right palm. With his left hand he gripped the handlebar. He pedaled the Spirit Flyer into the path of light. The whole family held hands, floating behind John like the tail of a kite. One by one, they entered the path of light that separated the darkness.

Just then, the hole in the giant's chest closed. He turned in rage, his black-gloved hand grabbing for the chain around Uncle Bill, who was last in line.

"Die!" the giant hissed.

But Uncle Bill entered the path of light. The giant screamed, drawing back his hand as if the light had burned him.

Then the whole family was inside the current of light, and the Spirit Flyer shot forward in a sweet note of deep music and Magic.

UNLOCKING THEIR CHAINS

· · · · · · · ·

22

The light bathed the family with a special, fresh feeling; it seemed something like the wetness of water. The old red bike and its passengers flowed forward in a fast current. Up ahead John saw a spot of blue. In no time they reached it, and the bike and its passengers popped out into a clear sky. They were high in the air over the old Centerville dump. John looked back just in time to see the white tunnel of light close and disappear in the blue sky. The path that came from the Deeper World was gone.

The old red bike kept flying fast. John held on tightly to Katherine's hand. The whole family was still holding hands. They seemed as light as balloons though the dark chains were on their necks. Their eyes were still closed.

The Spirit Flyer led them all away from Centerville. Before long it dropped down, circling over the weedy, overgrown yard of a white house with blue shutters. The house seemed abandoned. None of the windows were broken, but the paint was peeling. A long white building with two big blue doors stood next to the house.

The Spirit Flyer circled once more, then dropped lower, flying straight for the large blue doors. John feared they would crash, but as the old bike with the parade of prisoners flew closer, the big doors swung open. The Spirit Flyer glided inside, stopped in the air, then dropped softly to the cement floor. Katherine, Lois, Susan, Aunt Betty and Uncle Bill all landed on their feet.

John hopped off, letting go of Katherine's hand. The rest of the family still held hands, their eyes closed, their dark chains intact.

John shook Susan by her shoulder. His own chain rattled around his neck.

"Wake up, Susan!" John urged. But her eyes remained shut. "Uncle Bill? Aunt Betty? Lois? Katherine?"

Each one seemed to be in a deep sleep.

"What now?" John asked. The bike had landed in a kind of hallway. John decided to try a closed door.

"Maybe there's a telephone in there," John said. He opened the door. The room he entered was filled with boxes and crates covered with dust and cobwebs. John knew that some of the boxes had been opened recently; handprints marked the dust.

John worked his way through the boxes to a workbench against the far wall. He didn't see a phone. The boy leaned against the workbench, wondering what he should do, when he felt a piece of metal under his hand. He picked it up. The unusual shape interested him.

He brushed off the dust and looked closer. It was some sort of key, but where most keys had nicks and cuts and grooves, this key was flat and smooth. John examined the strange marks on it. He turned it over.

His eyes opened wide. Stamped in the gold-colored metal was the sign of the Three Crowns!

John ran back to the other room to tell his family, forgetting in his excitement that they were still chained, slaves of some kind of sleep or spell.

"Wake up! Wake up!" John called. "I have something from the Three Kings!" But they stood still like breathing statues.

John held up the key. At that instant there was a roar of deep music, and light filled the room. The Kramar family opened their eyes. They all saw the glorious Magic light that filled the place. John still held up the key. For one deep Magic moment, all six saw the wonders of the Kingdom of the Three Magical Kings. And from that deep Kingdom an arch of rainbow-colored light shot into the room and hit the golden key in John's hand. The light reflected off the key in six golden rays which disappeared into the circled-X locks on the chains. In a burst of music, the locks broke and the chains fell to the floor.

Just as suddenly as it came, the light was gone. The music faded into peaceful silence. For a moment, no one spoke; they could still feel the Magic glow.

"Where are we?" Katherine asked, rubbing her eyes. "At last we are safe."

"Look, it's John!" Susan shouted. She ran over and hugged his neck. John hugged her. Uncle Bill looked around the room. He was puzzled.

"Where are we?" Susan asked. "This place seems familiar somehow. Have I ever been here before?"

"Yes," Uncle Bill said. He rubbed his jaw slowly. "And so has John. In fact, John used to spend many hours here years ago. This is his father's old workshop. Actually, your Grandfather Kramar owns it. He said he would give it to John some day when John was ready. I never have understood what he meant."

Everyone was quiet. John looked at the others, then at the strange key in his hand.

"What happened?" Aunt Betty asked. "I thought we were at home. But something was wrong. A horrible dead smell was in the house. Then I had this bad dream."

"So did I," Uncle Bill said. "We were in this terrible . . . dark place."

"With a wall of blue flame," Lois said. "And all those mean creatures . . . Only some looked like people we know, sort of. But their faces were strange."

"They wore masks," Susan said. "I must have had the same dream too. We were at home and there was that bad smell. Then that . . . thing used the chains on our necks to put us into a tiny black box. We shrank. Then we went into that big . . . cloud or something."

"A giant black snake swallowed us," Katherine said. "It wasn't a cloud. The snake was evil and had red eyes."

"And red fangs," Aunt Betty added. "I guess I had the same dream you did. But how? I remember feeling scared, as if I were falling and falling into the mouth of that . . . snake. I thought it was a tornado at first. But I remember the chains. We couldn't escape."

"We were slaves," Uncle Bill said. "I must have dreamed the same dream too, only it was a nightmare. I didn't even notice my chain until we were in that black box. I still don't understand any of this. How did we get here?"

"Didn't you dream that too?" Lois asked. "We held hands. We went as fast as light out of that dark place because John's bicycle, the Spirit Flyer, took us."

"I remember screaming for John over and over," Susan said. "And those creatures said you were coming to save us. They said they would kill you when you came. Then they would kill all of us."

"And make us into ashes," Uncle Bill added. "But John, how did you get inside that . . . dark place?"

John told them as much as he remembered from the time he flew to Grandfather Kramar's house until the rainbow-colored light reflected off the key and freed them from their chains.

"And see, there are the chains," John said, pointing at the floor. "And this is the key. And here's your gun, Uncle Bill. I'm sorry the barrel got melted. But that proves it wasn't a dream. Maybe it was *like* a dream, but that's because it was part of the Deeper World."

Uncle Bill held the key and ruined gun with his hands. He shook his head slowly not saying a word. Then he reached down and picked up his chain.

"This chain has my name on it," Uncle Bill said. He ran his fingers over the letters.

"This chain has my name on it too," Susan said, picking up the chain at her feet.

"And so does mine," Lois said. "Look how big it is."

"Mine too," Katherine said.

Aunt Betty looked at her chain, then nodded. John held his chain, looking carefully at the broken circled-X lock.

I didn't even know I had a chain on me until that Daimone that looked like Barry Smedlowe wanted to fight," John said. "I felt real weak, like I would fall right off my bike. But the Spirit Flyer helped me."

A funny old horn tooted outside, followed by a chug-chug sound.

"Someone's coming," Lois said. "It sounds like a tractor." The whole Kramar family went outside.

"It's probably Salter Harper," Uncle Bill said. "His farm is near here."

They all stared at the dirt road that passed in front of the house. The chug-chug sound got louder, but no one came in sight.

"Look, it is a tractor!" John said. Instead of pointing at the road, he was pointing at the sky behind the house. Everyone looked. Uncle Bill's mouth fell open in disbelief.

"It's Grandpa!" Lois screeched. "And he's flying!"

Aunt Betty couldn't stop smiling as she watched the old red tractor chug over the rooftop and down onto the front lawn. As John and his cousins ran over to greet Grandfather Kramar, Aunt Betty squeezed her husband's hand. Uncle Bill finally smiled, staring hard into the eyes of his father. The old man winked back, then began showing his grand-

children the mysteries and wonders of the old tractor.

For more than two hours the children played on the old red tractor and John's bicycle. Grandfather Kramar even let John fly the tractor all by himself.

"Just be careful not to touch any of the gears or other buttons," the old man said. "And don't go out of the borders of this yard and that field. This is a special place."

While the children played, Grandfather Kramar, Uncle Bill and Aunt Betty talked, sitting on the porch steps of the house.

"But why didn't you ever show me or tell me?" Uncle Bill asked.

"I did. I took you for rides all the time when you were a child, but you forgot," the old man said. "And when you got older, you were never ready to listen or see. Today is the first time your eyes and ears have been open to the Deeper World. When those chains fell off, you were free. In more ways than one."

"I almost feel as if I remember flying on that old tractor now," Uncle Bill said. "But it's like a dream too. That was so long ago."

"We forget too many things about childhood," the old man said. "A child is ready for Magic, ready to hop right on a Magic bicycle and fly. In fact, let's enjoy the Magic we have right now," Grandfather Kramar said. "You don't have to be a child. Let's all take a ride on the Spirit Flyer Harvester. The harvest has been rich today. Let us ride and give thanks!"

Soon the whole family was hanging onto the old red tractor, screaming and giggling as Grandfather Kramar drove. They dipped and soared and looped in circles bigger than ferris wheels.

Time seemed to stop as they flew up and around and over the tiny farm of John's parents. Only Grandfather Kramar could see the long shadow shaped like a snake lingering just outside the fences that bordered the farm. He knew this shadow was not allowed to cross and darken the deeper joy of their rescue from the chains. And although he couldn't see them without his special goggles, he knew others were standing guard. He could hear their music.

MUCH TO
LEARN
ABOUT MAGIC

• • • • • • • •

23

They flew home just before the sun went down. Susan rode on the Spirit Flyer with John. The rest of the family rode with Grandfather Kramar on the old red tractor. Everyone felt tired, but full of life and peace, the way you feel after a day at the beach.

While they ate tomato soup and toasted cheese sandwiches, no one spoke. Grandfather Kramar knew it was good for them to think quietly about the rescue and the great things done.

When everyone finished eating, the old man finally spoke. "We need to talk."

But Katherine yawned. Then Aunt Betty yawned, followed by Susan. Then everyone yawned, even Grandfather Kramar.

"We need to stay awake and alert," the old man said. "This tiredness is a trick of theirs. We need to talk about the chains. We need to understand better what happened today."

"You mean we can't go to bed?" Lois asked. "I'm sleepy."

"That's right; it's bedtime," Uncle Bill said. "Just because we've had an *unusual* day doesn't mean the house rules change."

"Good," chimed in Katherine. "Because I'm tired too."

"Me too," yawned Susan. "I don't know when I've felt so tired."

"But we need to talk," the old man said. "Just for a while. We need to look at the chains. I have them here in the garage. They aren't ordinary chains. They can still be very dangerous."

"It's really getting late, Dad," Uncle Bill said. "I have house rules, and I don't think we should break them just because of those old chains. We can look at them tomorrow. You don't need to get back since Mom is still visiting Aunt Esther. We'll have plenty of time."

"I just need to show you a few things before we forget," Grandfather Kramar said. "We forget deep things like we forget dreams. Now is the time to hear and see."

"Tomorrow," Uncle Bill said. "Let's go to bed, all. Tomorrow we'll be fresher."

"I'd like to see the chains," John said. "And maybe we could look at those old bicycle instruments. Can we, Grandpa?"

"Well, if we can break some of these rules," the old man said weakly.

"I suppose you can stay up, if you want, John," Uncle Bill said slowly. "But just for a little while. You've had an even longer day than the rest of us. I guess from now on we can relax the rules from time to time. Maybe we should even change a few. But not tonight. It's bedtime."

Everyone left the room except Grandfather Kramar and John. The old man smiled, watching them leave.

"For a moment I thought he hadn't learned a thing," Grandfather Kramar said. "Change is always slow. Anyway, the kings work their Magic as they see fit. Let's go to the garage."

The cardboard box with the bicycle instruments was still on the work-bench where John had left it. Grandfather Kramar carefully handled the old broken light, the rubber horn, the generator, the gear lever and the rearview mirror.

"These are fine things," the old man said. "Fine, fine things in wonderful condition."

"But they're broken!" John exclaimed, surprised that his grandfather couldn't see that for himself.

"Of course they're broken," Grandfather Kramar said. "All things of Spirit Flyers are old and broken. But your bicycle has a lot of Magic, doesn't it?"

"Yes, I suppose," John said. "But why don't those kings make things that are nice and new? Things that last a little longer?"

"You have a lot to learn, boy," the old man said. "Someday you'll get an idea how old this bicycle is. Deep things last forever."

"But why is it all beat up and junky?" John asked. "I don't want to complain, really. I just don't understand."

"Look, boy," Grandfather Kramar said firmly, "if these instruments are broken, it's only because they *had* to be broken. And they had to be broken because *we* are broken. Don't you see that yet? You haven't even begun to know the wonders of this old *broken* bicycle. Can you imagine how hard it would be if these things *weren't* broken but new? You couldn't even stay seated on the Spirit Flyer, even strapped on with a steel seatbelt. You'd be blown away in the wind, burned up by the heat. All I'm saying is that if you want to become a good rider of this bicycle, you need to learn what you're sitting on and for what purposes."

"I guess there are lots of secrets I don't know," John said. He stroked the handlebars of the old red bike, feeling a dent.

"Well, as you keep riding, you'll understand why this bike was sent from the Deeper World to find you," Grandfather Kramar said. "You'll learn more about the Kingson and his Magic. But you can't learn it all in one day."

"We saw him," John said in a hushed voice. "In that room where the chains fell off, we saw him, Grandpa. He was in the light. I mean, the light was coming from him. I was too afraid to speak about him. None of us did. But we all saw. I hardly even want to talk about it."

"I know," the old man said. He patted John on the shoulder. "Sometimes we talk best inside our hearts, not out of our mouths. The kings hear."

The old man walked over to the tractor. He climbed up to get the chains. Then he frowned and sighed.

"I was afraid of that," he said sadly. He sighed again.

"What's wrong?" John asked.

"The chains are already gone," the old man said. "They've been stolen."

"What?" John asked. "But who could have stolen them?"

"The Daimones, of course," he said. "The slaves of the serpent. The ones you saw today."

"You mean like that giant Barry Smedlowe thing?" the boy asked. He looked around the garage fearfully, then ran over and got the slingshot off the handlebars of the Spirit Flyer.

"The damage is already done," the old man said wearily. "I just hoped it wouldn't have happened so soon. We lost that Magic moment when we could have looked at the danger. I wanted to show it to you all while the victory was still fresh. We'll have other chances, I'm sure, but I wish we wouldn't delay our lessons. Such a waste. Sometimes I forget how scared we are of the Magic of freedom." The old man shook his head, then climbed off the tractor.

"But why would the Daimones steal the chains?" John asked.

"So they can put them back on us," Grandfather Kramar said. "A person can still act like a slave, even though the locks are broken. The Daimones try to put broken chains back on their assigned people. They shadow them hard and whisper dead thoughts. Soon a person can believe he's a slave again when he isn't. The Tragic of the broken chains is powerfully dark and dangerous. We need to learn to keep the chains off."

John looked fearfully around the room. He held the slingshot. Then he remembered that last horrible face, just before he left the dark, dead world of the serpent.

"I saw something very odd in that dead place," John said. "Those Daimones looked like other children at school, like Barry Smedlowe. But right before we escaped, I saw one marching out of the darkness with the others . . . and he looked like me."

"Of course there's at least one assigned to you," Grandfather Kramar said. "We all have at least one. You probably have even more. Why do you think all these things have happened? Ever since the Spirit Flyer found you, the forces of the dark world have been afraid. That's why the tornado snake appeared so strongly to you. To frighten you away from Magic and keep you in chains. Don't forget, a war is going on in the Deeper World as it touches our world. Today was your first big battle and the forces of death lost. The Order of the Chains was weakened. But other battles will go on every hour of every day. So we must be open to the kings' Magic. You will learn as you ride the Spirit Flyer."

"It sounds kind of scary, but exciting too," the boy said as he looked at the wonderful old red bike. "Will the instruments help me? Can we put them on tonight?"

"The instruments make the Magic more complete," Grandfather Kramar said. "But let's look at them tomorrow. Tonight was the time to learn about the chains. You can't rush Magic. You don't run before you walk. And you aren't ready to even walk. You still need to sit on the Spirit Flyer and fly. You haven't yet learned patience. You jump off and fall through the roof, or you go off with a useless weapon of this world like your uncle's gun. You didn't put on the instruments as you were told; the Daimones tricked you that much."

"But I thought they were broken and no good," John said, trying to excuse himself. "How could I know they worked?"

"Because you were told and did know, deep inside," the old man said firmly. "The Spirit Flyer wouldn't have moved at all if you hadn't taken the slingshot. You wanted to leave it behind too, didn't you?"

"Yes," John said in a small voice. "I'm sorry."

"Don't be discouraged," Grandfather Kramar said. "We all make mistakes. You can only say you're sorry, then hop right back on that bike. Don't worry about what would have happened. That's the great thing about the kings' Magic; it's just our size, changing our failures into Magic. You'll learn, just like you're learning something important right now."

"What's that?" John asked.

"I'll let you think about it," the old man said, his eyes twinkling. "And we'll look at the instruments tomorrow. But remember, the kings only give the Magic as you have need. You can't rush it. You don't put on your shoes before your socks."

But John wasn't really listening. He stared at the cardboard box full of Magic instruments, suddenly greedy to try them out and use them. He wanted thrills and more Magic. He didn't see two deep hands slip his broken chain around his neck. The chain rested deep, invisible to him. But Grandfather Kramar could see the chain gleaming out of the boy's eyes, and he knew John would have to learn about the dangers of the chain from the kings. His words hadn't been enough to warn the young Magic flyer.

WHAT HAPPENED TO HORACE GRINSBY AND BARRY SMEDLOWE

· · · · · · · ·

24

On that same night, Barry Smedlowe was sucking on his last piece of Sweet Temptations candy and staring at the Kramar house. His father had given him strict orders to talk to Sheriff Kramar and apologize to John. But Barry had ridden his bicycle, the Goliath Cobra Deluxe, all around town for three hours, making excuses and wasting time.

"It's too late to see the sheriff now," Barry said, sitting in the shadows of a large tree. "I should have destroyed that trash-heap bike when I had the chance. I didn't really steal it. It was Grinsby's fault. If I'm going to get in trouble, he's going to be in trouble too. Big trouble. I wish I could see him right now. I'd show him."

"Show him what?" Horace Grinsby hissed, stepping from behind the tree.

"Aaaaag," Barry choked, swallowing the piece of Sweet Temptations.

"I think I'll show you something instead," Grinsby said. His eyes suddenly glowed red. Barry gasped. Then the figure with red eyes put his hands up to his ears and pulled forward, peeling off the face of Horace Grinsby. As the face came off, Barry screamed and shot out into the street on his bicycle.

He was halfway down the block when he looked back. Horace Grinsby's black truck was speeding down the street toward Barry. Two tiny red lights glowed behind the windshield.

Barry yelped and pedaled faster, jerking down on the Cobra gear lever. The wheels hummed in high gear, but the bike stopped moving. The tires turned round and round, burning into the pavement. Barry moaned and pedaled faster, but the tires just smoked and melted away. The front tire popped, then the rear. Thick black smoke surrounded Barry. Grinsby's truck squealed to a stop. The front door opened.

Barry jumped off the Cobra Deluxe, coughing from all the black smoke. He smelled something terrible and dead. The last thing he remembered before he passed out was two red eyes and a glowing red hook swinging toward his throat, a sound of metal hitting metal. Then everything was enveloped in the darkness of a nightmare.

Grinsby's black truck was roaring down the old dump road. The red telephone glowed on and off, but Grinsby refused to answer.

"It wasn't my fault," he said, trying to ignore the telephone. "I told you I needed more help. This boy made me fail. He's mine now."

The red phone glowed brighter and more rapidly. The figure snarled, then grabbed the phone and threw it out the window.

The phone exploded as it hit the road. Red flames shot high into the sky. The black truck was blown sideways into a ditch and stopped.

The explosion left a tower of smoke in the air. The smoke began to blow and swirl and twist into a deadly familiar shape. Two red eyes glowed out of the blackness. A mouth opened and a roaring hiss shook the ground.

"I refuse this punishment," the driver yelled. With tremendous force, he knocked the door off the truck and jumped out. He snarled again and shook the glowing red hook at the gigantic serpent.

A flash of lightning leaped from the serpent's mouth. As the lightning hit, the figure that had been Horace Grinsby glowed, then disappeared. All that remained was a tiny pile of ashes which were promptly sucked into the snake's mouth.

Then the snake turned toward the truck and spit fire again. But this time the lightning stayed in the air, a road of fire. The truck lifted up into the air and flew on the road of fire, disappearing into the darkness of the snake's mouth.

An explosion rocked Barry Smedlowe awake.

"Where am I?" Barry asked. He looked around fearfully. By moonlight he realized he was at the old dump outside town. On the ground next to him was his Goliath Cobra Deluxe. Both tires were melted. The wheels were bent and many spokes were broken. Barry remembered Grinsby's face and shivered.

He had been through a terrible nightmare. In the dream, he had traveled through the air in Grinsby's truck on a road of fire that led right into the mouth of a giant snake. The snake had swallowed him. Barry had felt suffocated because a huge chain had been locked around his throat. Something had happened inside the snake, but Barry couldn't remember quite what it was. He felt cold and empty. His mouth was dry, as if he'd been chewing ashes.

"But if it was a dream, how did I get way out here?" Barry asked. The mounds of trash looked like heaps of ashes in the pale moonlight. Barry shivered again. "I'm getting out of here."

He picked up his bike and noticed something different. A small, black metal box was bolted onto the handlebars right above the gear levers. A circled white X was on the side of the box. Somehow the box reminded him of his nightmare. But Barry was afraid to remember.

He quickly began pushing his bike into town.

"Boy, am I in trouble," he muttered. "They'll never believe me. And look at this trash-heap bike."

MAYBE
HE WENT
DEEPER
· · · · · · · ·
25

John lay in bed sleeping the next morning. A bird called outside his window. The boy felt a tug on his neck. The bird cried again, and at the same time another pull at his neck made him open his eyes. If he had been wiser to the ways of the Deeper World and of Tragic, he would have known the tug was his broken chain. But John still had much to learn.

"Might as well get a head start," he said, hopping out of bed. He quickiy dressed in his jeans, T-shirt and sneakers, then walked quietly out to the garage. He knew exactly what instrument he wanted to put on the old bicycle first: the gear lever. Gear levers meant speed, or so he figured. But John was rushing things. As soft as a dream, the Daimone pulled the chain harder, whispering, *"Faster, faster . . . how nice!"*

"Better hurry," John said. "So I can surprise everybody before breakfast."

John knew he should wait for his grandfather. Grandfather's last words had been, "Don't put on your shoes before your socks." But what was the harm in putting on one instrument? That way it would be ready when his grandfather got up. And the gear lever only had three positions. His old bike was a ten-speed, and he'd never had a problem with it, had he? John accepted all the excuses the Daimone whispered, making them his own.

Using the screwdriver and pliers, John quickly fastened the lever back onto the handlebars as he had found it. A wire cable ran from the gear lever, but ended, broken.

"It must attach to the rear sprocket," John said, dropping to his knees to inspect the back wheel. Sure enough, in the center of the back sprocket was a small lever with a hole in it.

"It must go right there," the boy said. He ran to his uncle's workbench and found a piece of wire. "Shoes before socks," a voice whispered in his mind. Although the wire seemed too thin, John decided to use it anyway. He was in a great hurry. He connected the wire to the gear cable, then ran it along the frame down to the back wheel. Within a minute he attached the wire to the small lever on the back sprocket.

"That should do it," John said, wiping the grease onto his pantleg. He heard noises inside the house. The family was awake.

"Just in time," John said, rolling the bicycle out the small garage door to the back yard. He pedaled slowly, then pointed the bike into the air. The Spirit Flyer glided smoothly above the ground. John leveled it off at three feet, then turned in the air, flying slowly back and forth across the lawn.

"Uncle Bill! Aunt Betty! Grandpa!" John yelled. "Come out back and see me! Quick, I'm going to try it out!"

Within ten seconds, the whole family, except Lois, came outside and stood on the patio next to the barbeque grill.

"Try out what?" Susan asked.

"I didn't hear him either," Uncle Bill answered.

"Surely he hasn't already put on . . ." Grandfather Kramar's voice died away as he saw the gear lever and the cable. "John, what have you—"

"Watch!" John shouted. At that instant, the boy pushed the gear lever with his finger. Something clicked. The whole family heard it. Then there was a hum, and as they watched, John faded, disappearing into the air.

"Wow! Did you see that?" Katherine asked.

"Oh, my," Aunt Betty cried. "Bill? Grandpa? Can't you do something?"

"Shoes before socks," Grandfather Kramar muttered. "I told that boy to be patient."

"What's happened, Dad?" Uncle Bill asked. "Will John be all right?"

"Sure, he'll be all right," the old man said.

"But are you *sure?*" Aunt Betty asked.

"Sure I'm sure. He's on the Spirit Flyer, isn't he? He won't hurt himself, though he might have to learn some hard lessons."

"So you know where he went?" Aunt Betty asked.

"Nope, I don't know that," the old man said, chuckling a bit. "Haven't got a clue. From what I saw, he didn't have that lever hooked up correctly. Shoes before socks, I warned that boy."

"Oh, Bill, what can we do?" Aunt Betty asked.

"You can't do a thing," Grandfather Kramar said. "But don't worry. He's all right. As I see it, he could have just done one of four things. He could have gone faster. That's the simplest, I suppose. Or he could have gone backward or forward."

"I have a feeling you don't mean backward or forward, like in a car," Uncle Bill said carefully.

"Nope, not like that," the old man said. "I mean backward or forward in time."

"Oh, Bill!" Aunt Betty cried. "You've got to . . . to stop him."

"How?" Uncle Bill asked.

"By . . . by . . . oh, Bill," Aunt Betty said softly.

"So he could have gone faster or backward or forward," Uncle Bill said. "That's only three. You said four."

"Well, I suppose he could have gone . . . deeper," the old man said. "Maybe he even went deeper backward, or deeper forward. I didn't really see how he had that gear lever hooked up."

"Deeper?" Aunt Betty said. "What's that? How do you mean, *deeper?*"

"Yes, how do you go deeper?" Uncle Bill asked.

"Let's go out to the tractor," Grandfather Kramar said. "I want to show you an old pair of goggles, and then I want you to try on a hat. You can listen to the story of Magic, and know what it means to go deeper."

So while the Kramar family sat around the old red tractor in the garage and learned about the story of Magic and the Deeper World, John was flying the Spirit Flyer on a new adventure known only to the kings.

John Bibee wrote The Magic Bicycle
while studying in Lima, Peru.
He currently lives in Austin, Texas,
with his wife and son.